"What are we doing?" Ludongo calls. "We're going down?"

Andrei answers, "The only way to avoid the storm is by penetrating the second cloud layer."

"But we're not supposed to go down for another two days! I have two days of experiments to do at this level!"

Bromley, "You can't arbitrarily juggle the mission plan like this without consulting us first. After all—"

"No time for discussion," Andrei cuts in. "We go down."

They're sore. And scared. Me too. Below the second cloud deck is the real unknown. Only a couple probes ever got back. Those sonar pictures. Big as mountains. And alive?

AS
ON A
DARKLING
PLAIN

BEN BOVA

AS ON A DARKLING PLAIN

A TOM DOHERTY ASSOCIATES BOOK
NEW YORK

AS ON A DARKLING PLAIN

Copyright © 1972 by Ben Bova

Portions of this book appeared in slightly different form in the following periodicals: "The Jupiter Mission" in the February 1970 issue of *Worlds of If* and "The Sirius Mission" in the January 1969 issue of *Galaxy*.

Published by arrangement with the author.

A Tor Book
Published by Tom Doherty Associates, Inc.
49 West 24th Street
New York, N.Y. 10010

Cover art by Tom Kidd

ISBN: 0-812-51546-3

First Tor printing: June 1985

Printed in the United States of America

0 9 8 7 6 5 4 3 2

CONTENTS

The universe is not only queerer than we imagine—it is queerer than we *can* imagine.
—J.B.S. HALDANE

Clarke's Third Law: Any sufficiently advanced technology is indistinguishable from magic.
—ARTHUR C. CLARKE

Deep in cryogenic sleep the mind dreams the same frozen dreams, endlessly circuiting through the long empty years. Sidney Lee dreamed of the towers on Titan, over and again, their smooth blank walls of metal that was beyond metal, their throbbing, ceaseless, purposeful machines that ran at tasks that men could not even guess at. The towers loomed in his darkened dreams, standing menacing and alien above the frozen wastes of Titan, utterly unmindful of the tiny men who groveled at their base. He tried to scale those smooth steep walls, and fell back. He tried to penetrate them, and failed. He tried to scream, and—in his dreams, at least—he succeeded.

1. TITAN

Lee looked down at his gloved hands. They were shaking uncontrollably, as if they belonged to someone else and he had no power over them at all.

He was standing on an ice bluff, overlooking the plain where the towers stood. Even from this distance they seemed to pulsate, to glow with unknown energies. He could feel the machines inside them throbbing, rumbling, endlessly, always at work. Always. A tiny knot of pressure-suited men huddled along the base of one of the buildings, insectlike and insignificant at this distance. The towers soared above them, probing straight and alien into the dark sky of Titan. A column of tracked cars inched along the icy plain toward the towers. More insects.

The fat, gaudy crescent of Saturn hung overhead, its rings just a thin, barely visible line, like the border between sanity and madness. Somewhere Lee could hear laughter, alien laughter, disdainful and completely superior.

There were five people working with him. With their pressure suits on, they too looked like clumsy beetles clambering painfully over the frozen wasteland, going through instinctive motions while the builders of those towers watched from far, far off, pointing at the pitiful men of Earth and laughing.

Lee walked away. He didn't say a word, he just started walking. It was several minutes before any of the others realized that he was leaving them. Had left them.

"Dr. Lee?"

"Dr. Lee, where are you going? Shall we . . ."

"Sid! What's wrong?"

"Can you hear us? Answer please!"

He touched a switch on the belt of his pressure suit and their voices snapped off. It was always dark on Titan, walking alone was discouraged. But Saturn's crescent cast enough light so that Lee didn't bother to turn on his helmet lamp. Even when a wispy ammonia cloud drifted across the yellowish crescent, Lee kept right on walking.

Faster and faster, down the gentle back slope of the ice bluff, cleated boots crunching into the frozen ground. His pace quickened as he went downhill, the walk became a trot, then a full run.

He raced over the tumbled ice with huge, loping, low-gravity strides, straight toward the edge of the ammonia sea. The faceplate of his helmet fogged, his ears ached with the sound of his own thundering pulse. But he kept on, lungs rasping, sweating, eyes stinging, running for the sea.

It might have taken an hour or a few minutes. Lee didn't think about the time. He stopped at the shore of the gray sea of ammonia. Colder than any ice-filled ocean of Earth, the ammonia sea was ruled by Saturn's immense tidal pull; it slid foaming, churning, breaking against the cliffs a hundred kilometers away and then back again, halfway up the ice bluff. The tide was coming in now. In a quarter hour, maybe less, the purifying ammonia would cover Lee with twenty meters of silent, cold darkness.

He stood and waited, watching the current lapping closer, covering this mound of ice, that shard of rock, edging up to his boots, swirling around the bright metal leggings of his pressure suit.

Five years, he thought. *Five years today. It took me five years to admit it. We'll never know. The towers will always defeat us.*

Some instinct made him turn his head. Through the plastic bubble of his helmet he could see three people racing, tumbling down the slope, heading toward him. They were waving their arms, gesticulating wildly. *Probably shouting themselves hoarse,* he thought.

Unhurried, Lee looked back at the sea. *Not enough time. They'll get here first.*

Very deliberately and carefully, he reached up to the neck of his pressure suit and began to unfasten the seal.

Man reached toward the stars not in glory, but in fear.

The buildings on Titan were clearly the work of an alien, intelligent race. No man could tell exactly how old they were, how long their baffling machines had been running, what their purpose was. Whoever had built them had left the solar system hundreds of centuries ago.

For the first time, men dreaded the stars.

Still, they had to know, had to learn. Robot probes were sent to the nearest dozen stars, the farthest that man's technology could reach. A generation passed on Earth before the faint signals from the probes returned. Seven of the stars had planets circling around them. Of these, five possessed Earth-like worlds. On four of them, some indications of life were found. Life, not intelligence.

Long and hot were the debates about what to do next. Finally, it was decided to send manned expeditions to all four of the Earth-like planets.

Through it all, the machines on Titan hummed smoothly.

2. EARTH:

The Sequoia Forest

They had hiked well away from the main trail, carrying their bulky backpacks across the uneven ground, gawking at the huge sequoia boles that stood straight and solemn as pillars in a cathedral. Bob O'Banion was tall, broad-shouldered, fair-haired, smiling, and young. Marlene Ettinger was tall for a woman, leggy in hiking shorts, strong in a completely feminine way.

A bird swooped past them and Bob laughed and pointed. The mottled sunshine filtering through the branches so far overhead set off sparkling highlights in Marlene's long, auburn hair. They walked in silence, only an arm's reach apart, yet separated.

She watched his face as they walked. He was happy, happy to be away from training, to be out of uniform, happy to forget about the buildings on Titan and the star missions, happy to be in the forest soaking up the sun's warmth and smelling the piney odor of the redwoods and listening to the sounds of life. Soon enough they would all be locked into metal wombs for the long journey. And sooner still she would have to tell him. . . .

"Here's a good place," Bob said.

It was a flat, mossy spot between giant trees. A cold stream sluiced by, making barely a sound. A squirrel chittered at them briefly from the fire-hollowed base of a sequoia. When they didn't leave, the squirrel dashed out of sight.

Marlene nodded and gratefully let the heavy backpack slide off her shoulders. Bob braced his pack against a tree trunk and pulled out an old-fashioned blanket. Not a plastic spread or even a synthetic fabric: an honest, faded blue fuzzy wool blanket.

She smiled at him.

"What's funny?"

"Nothing. I didn't realize you were such a traditionalist."

He grinned back at her as he bent over the pack and took out food packages. "There's a lot you don't know about me. Yet."

She kept the smile on her face. But behind it she was asking, *And can't you realize that there's so much about me that you don't know?*

They ate, they talked. Inevitably the conversation drifted to the buildings on Titan, to the upcoming star missions, to their training. Inevitably they finished eating and lay down on the yielding ground side by side. And soon he was holding her, touching her, kissing her.

"Bob," she said, "when I was on Titan . . ."

"I don't want to talk about Titan or anything else," he murmured in her ear.

"No . . . I've got to tell you." She pushed away slightly. His youthful face clouded for an instant, but then he smiled and said, "Marlene, you don't have to. . . ."

"Yes, I do," she said. She sat up, then turned to look back at him. "I saw a man try to kill himself on Titan. He just walked off into the sea one day. We barely got to him in time. He was unlocking his helmet when we reached him."

Bob made a sympathetic noise.

"You see . . . I was in love with him. He was married, but his wife had stayed on Earth, and we . . ." Her voice trailed off.

His smile died. "But I thought you and me . . . we've got something good going between us, Marlene."

"I know. Honestly, I thought I had forgotten him, that what happened on Titan was all over . . . but yesterday I saw him again. He's at the Training Center now, trying to qualify for a star mission."

"And you still love him?"

She could see the pain in his eyes. "Bob, I don't know. Until yesterday you were the only man I cared about. But now—he didn't even see me, I only caught a glimpse of him as he got off the shuttle. . . ."

"Maybe you were mistaken. Maybe it isn't him."

"No. I checked. It's him. He's been in the hospital for more than a year, but now he's at the Training Center. It's him."

"And you and me?" Bob asked. "What happens to us?" The pain had reached his voice now.

"I don't know," she answered, her voice barely a whisper. "I don't know if he's the same person he was on Titan. Maybe he doesn't want me now. Maybe he never really loved me. I just don't know."

The pain had reached her long ago.

3. EARTH:

The Training Center

It looked like a campus. Big plastiglass buildings with swooping curved roofs and graceful rampways connecting them at every tenth level. Trees that still looked new and gawky as they poked thin leaves into the burning Texas sky. Grass kept green by underground irrigation so that the forty thousand men and women of the Training Center would have pleasant lawns to stroll past or lunch on.

Forty thousand people. Eighty of them would go to the stars.

Marlene rode the lift up to the twenty-eighth level, shivering slightly from the too-efficient air conditioning. The car slid to a smooth, quiet halt and the doors slid open noiselessly. In mid-morning, the dormitory hallway was empty of people. The walls were bare and antiseptic white. Like a hospital.

She started down the hall in one direction, hesitated, reversed herself. Walking slowly, she read the names on each identical plastic door until she came to LEE, S., PhD

For a moment she stood before the door, uncertain. Then she touched the buzzer.

No answer.

She wondered whether to ring again or forget the whole thing. Abruptly, the door pulled open and Sidney Lee stood there facing her.

"Marlene!" He looked surprised.

"Hello, Sid."

He was thinner, his face all bone and tendon, his eyes faintly haunted. Hair still dark, just a touch of gray.

"Uh . . . come on in." He gestured. "What are you doing up here?"

She stepped into his room. "You never answered my messages, so I decided to come and see what's keeping you so busy." She tried to make it sound light, pleasant.

The room was small, functional, sterile. Morning sunlight at the only window. A foam couch, desk, wall drawers, two sling chairs. Doors that must have closets and bathroom and kitchen behind them. No decorations, no personal touches, no warmth.

Standing beside her, Lee pointed to the gray

computer terminal box on the desk. "That's what's been making a hermit out of me. I'm a schoolboy again."

She smiled at him.

"I've got a lot of studying to do," he explained, "to qualify for a star mission. There's a lot I've got to learn."

"It keeps us all busy," she said quietly.

They stood next to each other in the middle of the flat, impersonal room, the room he lived in, the room they had given him.

"I know," he admitted. "I should have answered your calls. . . ."

"It's all right, Sid. I just wanted to make sure you . . . you're all right. If you're busy, I can leave."

"No, don't go. . . . Here, sit down, I'll get some coffee."

So she sat in one of the sling chairs and toyed with the gold medallion that Bob had given her while Lee fidgeted noisily in the kitchen. He came out shaking his head, carrying two steaming mugs.

"I hope my qualification exams don't include mechanical aptitude," he said, handing her a cup. "I have a battle with that damned coffeemaker every day."

He pulled the other chair up next to her and sat in it.

She asked, "How have you been? We were so worried about you."

"They gave me a clean bill of health at the hospital."

She sipped at the coffee. It was too strong, and hot enough to hurt her teeth.

"You look just fine, Marlene. What have you been doing since they carried me off Titan?"

He said it flatly, without a smile or a grimace. But she thought she saw something in his eyes.

"I've been there all the while. Until a few months ago, that is. When they started the star flight program, I volunteered, and they sent me here."

He nodded.

"I tried to get in touch with you from Titan," she said. "But the hospital wouldn't permit it."

"I didn't know. . . ."

"Do you think we'll be placed on the same star mission?"

He shrugged. They sat looking at each other for an agonizingly long, silent moment.

Marlene finally said, "There's a rumor going around the Center that you were offered the job of chief of the archaeology section on Mars, but you turned it down."

"That's right. I want a star flight, not Mars."

"But—head of the section . . ."

"There's nothing for me on Mars," he said gravely. "They only asked me because of the Martian script business. That's all ancient history now. The man who deciphered the script. That's the bag they want to keep me in. A nice safe position.''

"But it's an honor, Sid. They didn't have to—''

"Look,'' he snapped. "I deciphered all ninety-six lines of the script. They want me to sit in a dome up there and wait for somebody to find more? A few more scratches dug out of sand? Let somebody else read it.''

Anger! Why is he angry?

"Once you've seen those machines,'' he went on, his face grim, "once you've *felt* them going night and day, every minute, every year . . . everything else is meaningless. You know that.''

"Everything?'' she asked.

He looked straight at her. "Everything. Why do you think I've been living inside this room for two weeks straight, trying to cram my head full of all the things I'll need to know to qualify for a star mission?''

"But you don't have to. . . .''

"Yes I do!'' His voice was tense, urgent. "I've got to do better on these qualification tests than anybody else in the Center. I've got to do so well that they won't have the slightest excuse for turning me down. I've got to qualify! I've got to get on a star flight! Nothing else matters.''

"But you will, Sid. They couldn't possibly turn you down.''

His eyes were blazing now. "Couldn't they?

The chief administrator's already asked me to take the Mars job, to quit the Training Center.''

"He has?"

"Not in so many words . . . but I know what he wants. He's afraid of putting me on a starship. Afraid I might crack up again, light-years out where they can't do anything about it. Afraid I'll wreck the mission and kill everybody.''

"That's cr—'' She caught herself too late.

Pointing at her, "See what I mean? Once you get the tag, it doesn't wear off. They're really afraid of me. They'd much rather see me quit the star program. Or flunk out.''

"You say the chief administrator told you?''

He nodded. "Know what my answer was? I told him that there are only eight archaeologists in the whole star program. He's going to need four of them at least. I told him that if he forced me out, I'd get all eight of them to resign in protest.''

"You didn't! What did he say?''

"What could he say? He changed the subject.''

"You'd really do that, Sid? You'd ask them all to quit?''

"Damned right. And they'd do it for me. I know they would. I'd *make* them do it for me!''

Then Marlene suddenly heard herself asking, "And your wife? How does she feel about a star flight?''

He hesitated for only a fraction of a second.

"We're divorced. As soon as I got out of the hospital."

"Oh . . ." She had guessed it long ago, and hated herself for bringing it up. "I'm sorry, Sid. I didn't mean to pry."

He was facing her, but his eyes were seeing something else, something that hurt. "It ended a long time ago," he said woodenly. "Before I went to Titan, I guess. It's just that . . . well, it didn't end gracefully. There was a lot of fighting at the end. My fault, mostly."

"Don't blame yourself . . ."

"Who else?" He pulled himself out of the chair and took the half-empty cup from her hand. "Here, I'll get you some more."

"No, let me." Marlene struggled up out of the sling chair. It wasn't easy to do in one graceful motion.

He was already halfway to the kitchenette. "I'll get it," he called over his shoulder.

She stood there, uncertain, hating the part of herself that was glad he was no longer married, even though it hurt him so much.

The phonescreen chimed.

"Answer!" he called out.

"Dr. Lee," said a computer's carefully modulated voice while the viewscreen stayed blank, "you asked to be reminded within a half hour of your appointment with the psychiatric clinic. It is now ten thirty. Your appointment is at eleven, in building—"

"I know. Turn off."

Lee stared at her for a moment, then turned and started fussing with the coffeemaker.

"Psychiatric exam," he said without looking up at her. "I get them every week, to see how I'm handling the pressure of the Training Center. That's just a little something extra they've thrown at me. If they find anything in those exams that they can use against me, I'll be out the door ten minutes later."

"Oh, Sid, they wouldn't . . ." She started toward him in the kitchenette.

"Wouldn't they?" He still wasn't looking at her; he was punching buttons along the base of the cooking unit and rattling the coffeemaker with his other hand. "You'd be surprised what they can do. Like having Sylvia pop in on me for an unannounced visit. To see what my reactions are. Shock treatment."

Marlene felt her mouth drop open.

"Nice people. Thorough . . ." He jiggled the coffeemaker, banged it, then—with a growl of rage—tore it out of the cooker element and banged it against the kitchen wall. Coffee splattered everywhere as the fiber container burst. Marlene jumped back and still got some splashed on her, hot but not searing. Lee stood in the middle of the kitchenette alcove, the metal handle broken off in his hand, dripping coffee.

"Can't you see how much I've got pounding on me?" he shouted at her. "How the hell can I even *talk* to you with all this on me? That's why I didn't answer your calls. It's too much. All of it! Too much!"

"But Sid, I want to help you, to—"

"*No!* Leave me alone. What we had on Titan is over with, Marlene. I don't know where I am now, or where I'm going. You've got to . . . just . . . leave me alone!"

She turned, eyes filling with tears, and ran from the room.

4. EARTH:

The End of The Day

They sat facing each other across a narrow table.
Outside their booth, the bar was crowded with
couples dancing, drinking, laughing, talking. Bob
had put up the silence screen, so none of the noise
penetrated into their booth. The rest of the world
was just a frenetic pantomime of flashing colors
and meaningless, foolish people who postured and
gestured like mute puppets.

She seemed down: not just physically tired, emo-
tionally drained. But Bob O'Banion hardly noticed
Marlene's looks, in his own turmoil.

"I've been assigned to the Jupiter mission," he
said.

Her eyes widened. "Not a star flight?"

"No," he answered flatly. "I'm not good enough

for that." He felt cold inside, the kind of helpless anger that leaves you feeling numb. As if he, the *real* Bob O'Banion, was someplace far distant and looking back on this scene, watching, detached, alone, walled off from all human contact.

"You shouldn't think of it that way," Marlene was saying.

"They're going to send me to another training center. I spent the afternoon finding out about it. They'll do things to my body, so I can live in a high-pressure liquid environment. They'll take out my lungs and put plastic gills in my throat. They'll rearrange the muscles in my legs and web my toes. They'll—"

She clapped her hands over her ears. "No! Bob, don't."

He went on, emotionlessly, watching her cower under his words. "They claim they'll put me back together again after the mission. If I live through it. Be the same afterwards, hardly a scar. By the time you come back from your star flight I'll be more than ninety years old."

"Don't do it," she said. "Don't let them do it to you."

"Why not? It's an important mission. And they'll kick me out if I don't volunteer for it."

"They're forcing you?"

"That's what they need me for. It's either Jupiter or resign."

"Then quit!" Marlene said. "There's no need for you to—"

"Will you quit too?" he asked suddenly. "Will you come with me, wherever I'm going, and forget everything else?"

For a shocked moment she said nothing. Then, "I . . . Bob, I can't." Her voice was barely audible.

He took a deep breath. "Your . . . friend. He's going on a star mission? He's been accepted?"

"I don't know."

"He'll be accepted. You'll go on the same ship."

"Bob . . . he doesn't care about me. Not anymore. He's got enough problems without me hanging on him."

"Then come with me. To hell with the damned machines on Titan. Let somebody else worry about them."

"I can't."

"Why?"

"Bob, try to understand. I'm a person. I've got a career. I spent three years on Titan and now I have an opportunity to go on a star mission. Only a handful of people have that chance. . . .'

"I'm willing to give up my career for you," he said.

She said nothing, avoided his eyes.

"Okay. That's it, then."

She reached out and touched his arm. "Don't go, Bob. Don't let them do this to you."

"Don't let *them*?" He nearly laughed.

She didn't understand. "Don't let them send you to Jupiter. Not if you don't want to go. Not if they're going to turn you into . . . into . . ."

"I'm going."

"But the psychologists won't pass you if they find out. . . ."

He did laugh now. "The psychologists! Do you know how many people they've gotten to volunteer for this thing? They're down on their knees begging for two or three scientists. Us military types they can order to volunteer. They're not worried about psychological attitudes. They're scared of those buildings on Titan and they want us to poke into Jupiter and see if anybody pokes back. It's a suicide mission."

He slid out of the booth, into an explosion of sound: raucous music, shouting voices, jostling, laughing people. As he pushed toward the door, he looked back at Marlene. She sat in her web of silence. Now she was completely alone.

Two years went quickly. Training, studying, struggling, worrying. Giant ships were assembled in orbit around Earth. More than a million people on the mother planet and the Moon worked to prepare for the flights of exploration. The flights of fear.

And then the ships were gone. Four of them went toward the stars. Four more to Jupiter, although only one of them would actually attempt to penetrate the giant planet's swirling clouds.

The two years were not without mishap. There were accidents. There were disasters. People died. Men quit the program when they couldn't take any more. Others were quietly dismissed when they couldn't measure up to the necessary standards.

And still others—six men, a handful—were surgically altered to face the rigors of Jupiter.

5. THE JUPITER MISSION

I am the ship.

We're cruising okay now, just under the cloud deck. Wind velocity outside still brutal, gusty. Makes us buck and shudder like a glider in a thunderhead. My infrared eyes see the ammonia clouds above us as cold and gray. Lots of turbulence.

Took a helluva beating getting through the clouds. Scientists must've been scared. So was I on that one jolt. It hurt.

Snowing like hell all around us. I can barely see the second cloud layer, 'way below. Looks vaguely pinkish, warm. They're supposed to be water clouds, ice crystals. And below that? Intelligent life? The people who built the machinery on Titan?

Captain's snoozing. I am the ship. Me. Robert Donovan O'Banion. All alone except for the computer and this recorder I'm mumbling into. The scientists are plugged into their special instruments, each of them in his own narrow cubicle. But I'm the *ship*. Plugged in completely. The engines are my heartbeat. Computer flashes information in my eyes and talks right into my brain. The recorder takes down this subvocal chatter for the ship's log. I see outward with infrared or sonar or any of the other sensors. And inward with the intercom cameras. I'm in touch with every piece of machinery, every electrical circuit, every transducer and sensor. They all plug into me.

Me. The human me. I can see myself: floating in a contour couch like some enlarged fetus, naked and depilitated, gills flapping softly. Body bobbing gently in the currents that surge through this heavy saline solution we live in. Face mostly hidden behind sensory connectors and communications unit. Cranial connectors pressed against bald skull like a yarmulke. Hands and feet enclosed in more sensory connectors and control units.

A semi-mechanical fetus, breathing liquid with manmade gills. A part-time cyborg.

SYSTEMS REPORT. ALL SYSTEMS PERFORMANCES AT NOMINAL VALUES. ALL SYSTEMS WITHIN TOLERABLE LIMITS.

I don't know why they used my voice for the computer's vocal output. It doesn't even sound like me, anyway. The captain laughs about it; says it's like I'm talking to myself. At least they didn't try to build a personality into the computer. Four scientists aboard is enough personality for any mission.

What's Ling saying?

"They are definitely biological. Look at the readouts yourself."

Intercom camera view. Ling's sitting on the edge of his couch. It's cranked up to sitting position and swiveled to his workbench. He's flashing the readout from one of his instruments over the intercom. The spectrophotometer. It's a list of numbers. The recorder will read it off for the data file. Other three scientists are making professional grunts and grumbles.

"Highly reduced hydrocarbons, for the most part," Ling goes on. "But notice, please, lines fourteen and thirty-seven: leucine and tyrosine. Amino acids."

Ling's trying to maintain his Chinese cool, but he sounds excited. Check his medical monitor. Yep . . . heart rate's up.

"Amino acid molecules," Bromley says flatly from his cubicle. "We're in the midst of a biological blizzard."

No surprise. The unmanned probes discovered the biological "snow" falling from the top cloud deck. Sunlight and lightning drive biochemical reactions in the clouds; amino acids and other gunk precipitates out. It's what happens to the stuff underneath the second cloud deck that we're supposed to investigate.

Shame Ling's depilitated. He'd look better with a stringy moustache. The compleat Chinese sage. Head too big for his skinny body. Bromley's just the opposite: soft and round. I swear he's bloating. He looks spongier every time I check on him. He can't be gaining weight on what we get for nutrients!

Ludongo's hunched over his instruments, running tests on the gas samples we've sucked in. "Doc" Speer's hanging onto his couch; hasn't said a word since the first jolt up in the clouds. Youngest man aboard. Hope to Christ we don't have a medical emergency. He'd be useless.

COMMUNICATIONS CHECK. The computer flashes the words before my eyes as well as saying them to me.

Okay, sweep the radio frequencies. . . . Nothing, just nerve-sizzling interference. The electrical storms make everything useless. Try the laser again. Won't go through the clouds. All right, end communications check. We're cut off from the orbiting ships, completely shut away from the rest of the human race. Not even the starships are this alone.

SHIP SYSTEMS CHECK.

Now the computer's flashing data at me, images flickering in my eyes as fast as my brain can take in the information: propulsion systems, electrical power, life support, structural integrity . . . numbers, bar charts, symbols, graphs, curves. Outside pressure's up to ten atmospheres. And we've just started. When do we enter the second cloud deck?

IN FORTY-SIX HOURS EIGHTEEN MINUTES ACCORDING TO MISSION PLAN.

Below that deck is the ocean, where the pressure *starts* at a ton per square centimeter. Then we'll see how good a ship we are.

Were those sonar pictures from the unmanned probes really showing animals? As big as icebergs?

Ludongo's floated into Ling's cubicle. They're comparing notes. Ludongo's got his atmospheric analysis finished, looks like. And Ling's working on the biochemistry of the snowflakes.

Hah! Bromley's getting off his ass and joining them. Can't have the nonwhites plotting together.

Ling's saying, "It's amazing how similar the biochemistry is to the terrestrial pattern."

Bromley floats in and grabs a handhold. The cubicle's barely big enough for the three of them. Ludongo nods hello and drifts behind Ling's couch to the corner where the medical monitoring console is housed. Maybe I ought to make them stay in their own cubicles and chat over the intercom. If we hit more turbulence . . .

Check the outside infrared. Give me a course plot and turbulence prediction.

NO MAJOR TURBULENCE WITHIN INSTRUMENTS' RANGE AND SENSITIVITY.

Okay. Let them float around for a while. Bulkheads are padded. Alert me if any sign of turbulence shows up.

UNDERSTOOD.

My God, Speer's getting up! Finally getting a little courage, or is he scared of being alone?

DISTURBANCE DETECTED AT MAXIMUM INFRARED RANGE.

Show me. Humph . . . flickering light. Gone now. No, there's another. Give me max magnification. Must be a lightning storm. Distance?

DATA INSUFFICIENT FOR DISTANCE ESTIMATE.

Hell! Looks pretty dim, but infrared wouldn't pick up much of a lightning bolt, would it? No ideas at all for estimating the distance?

COMPARISON OF VISUAL SIGNAL AGAINST AUDIBLE SIGNAL COULD GIVE APPROXIMATION OF DISTANCE.

Listen for the boom, yeah. Like we used to do when we were kids, gauge the distance to a thunderstorm. Turn on the outside mikes and filter out the boundary layer and background noise. What's the speed of sound out there?

BASED ON MEASUREMENTS OF ATMOSPHERIC PRESSURE AND COMPOSITION, SOUND SPEED IS APPROXIMATELY SIX KILOMETERS PER SECOND PLUS OR MINUS TWENTY PERCENT.

But I don't hear anything. No boom. Shock

waves must be damping out. What's the damping function for this atmosphere?

DATA INSUFFICIENT FOR ESTIMATE.

Great. Now do I let them stand around and jabber or do I send them back to their couches?

NO MAJOR TURBULENCE PREDICTED FOR AT LEAST THIRTY MINUTES.

Inside view. Speer's bobbing softly in the passageway just outside Ling's compartment, one hand on the open hatch. The others are jammed inside.

Ling's saying, "If this biological snow is falling all across the planet, what happens to it in the second cloud layer, I wonder? And in the ocean?"

"Torn to shreds, I should imagine," says Bromley. "Those are not the warm, gentle seas of Earth down there, you realize. They're no doubt highly corrosive, laced with plenty of ammonia and God knows what else. Long-chain molecules simply wouldn't have a chance in that ocean."

Ludongo looks like he's fed up with Bromley's pompousness, but Ling just smiles like a cat.

"Indeed?" Ling asks softly. "But what of the sonar pictures that the probes returned? What of those huge objects floating in the ocean?"

"Icebergs, rocks, mountains torn loose from the surface below . . ."

"So? *Warmer* than the ambient seas around them?"

Bromley's looking uncomfortable. "I'll admit that there's a good deal we have to learn. But one shouldn't jump to conclusions. Whoever built those machines on Titan certainly did not come from Jupiter . . . nor from Saturn, for that matter. Any fool could have told the politicians that.''

Ludongo's father is a politician. He says, ''Yes, of course. But if we convinced the politicians of that fact, there would have been no Jupiter mission at all.''

''Frankly, I wouldn't have minded a bit,'' Bromley says. ''This is no place for a manned expedition. Unmanned probes could do everything that needs to be done here. I volunteered for a star mission, not this. I accepted Jupiter because they needed me.''

''We all desired star missions.'' Ling smiles sadly.

''And none of us qualified,'' adds Speer.

''I qualified for a star mission,'' Ludongo counters. ''But my father, the Prime Minister''—he stares straight at Bromley—''did not want me to go. By the time I returned even from Alpha Centauri he would be long in his grave.''

''Yet he permitted you to go on this . . . this . . .'' Bromley means *suicide mission*.

''A Ludongo does not back away from a question of courage.''

Speer hunches his thin shoulders. ''Let's face it. We're expendables. For this mission they needed good capable men who wouldn't be missed too much if they didn't come back.''

He made three great friends with that crack. We all know it's true, but who wants to admit it? The only nonexpendable member of this mission is the recorder. It listens to everything we say, takes down every bit of data from the instruments, carries my muttering for the log. They built it to get back to the orbiting ships all by itself, even if we break into pieces.

Starting to hear rumbles from the lightning storm. Bolts getting bright enough to blank out my eyes for a split second.

MODERATE TURBULENCE TEN MINUTES AHEAD.

Noted. . . . Hey, there's a blast! Single lightning tree zapping from the clouds above all the way down to the second deck.

SEVERE TURBULENCE THIRTY SECONDS AHEAD.

"Grab onto something quick!" I holler into the intercom.

Turn off the outside mikes. Oof! Like getting hit with a hammer. Stabilizer cuts in. Okay.

Inside camera. "Everybody all right?"

They're grumbling and swearing. Nobody hurt.

"Get back to your own couches and strap in. Strong turbulence coming up."

How come you gave only a thirty-second warning?

ELECTRICAL STORM GROWING RAPIDLY. GROWTH PARAMETERS INSUFFICIENTLY

UNDERSTOOD FOR DETAILED TURBULENCE
PREDICTION.

Thanks for admitting it . . . after the fact. Storm's
spreading and we're heading right into it. *Car-
penter's* not much on maneuvering; more like a
dirigible than a rocket craft.

Here's Captain Voronov. Chunky Russian. Used
to be blond and jovial. Looks worried now. Buck-
les himself into the pilot's couch and fits the connectors to face and cranium.

Now there are two of us. He's sharing the ship
with me. He slips his hands and feet into the
control connectors. We're linked.

"Don't think we can get around it, Andy."

I can sense him nodding. My eyes are watching
the flickering lightning, closer than ever now. The
computer's superimposing numbers over the outside view: storm's extent, our course and speed,
turbulence levels.

"I would not care to try going through it,"
Andrei says. His English comes out slow and
careful, in a deep baritone. This saline we live in
makes everybody's speech a bit slower and deeper
than normal.

The scientists are all battened down, like good
little boys. They're watching their display screens,
looking at the storm.

"Would it be possible," Ling asks softly, "to
get close enough to the storm to observe the effect
of the lightning on the biological particles?"

"Lord, I should hope not," says Bromley.

"Too much turbulence," Andrei says firmly.

He's checking the mission plan and our performance limits. I get it. He wants to dive *under* the storm, through the second cloud deck! I run a systems check and start the computer plotting an optimum maneuver.

"Good, Robert," Andrei says as the course plot flashes before our eyes. "The descent rate is steep, but within tolerable limits. Execute."

It is steep! My stomach doesn't like it. Displays are flashing like a movie show now: engine thrust, temperatures, hull pressures, strain, descent rate . . .

Listen to them wail!

"What are we doing?" Ludongo calls. "We're going down?"

Andrei answers, "The only way to avoid the storm is by penetrating the second cloud layer."

"But we're not supposed to go down for another two days! I have two days of experiments to do at this level!"

Bromley, "You can't arbitrarily juggle the mission plan like this without consulting us first. After all—"

"No time for discussion," Andrei cuts in. "We go down."

They're sore. And scared. Me too. Below the second cloud deck is the real unknown. Only a couple probes ever got back. Those sonar pictures. Big as mountains. And alive?

We're really bouncing now. I can feel liquid gurgling in my ears. Outside view a blank; we're in the clouds. Damned couch feels like it's got rocks in the padding. Straps cutting into me. Ship feels okay, though: engines strong. Bright boys in back are clammed up. Woop . . . was that Bromley's yell? Don't blame him. Another drop like that and I'll yell too.

Starting to ease off, I think. Maybe we . . . *ow!* What was that?

YELLOW ALERT. SUBSYSTEM MALFUNCTION. GENERATOR OUTPUT DOWN TEN PERCENT.

"Check it," Andrei says to me.

Performance graph doesn't look too bad. No real danger. Look into the generator bay. Everything seems normal . . . wait. A bubble just drifted up from back behind the . . . get a close-up. Yep, a leak in the coolant line. Nothing serious. Not yet.

"I see it," Andrei says.

Ship's riding smoother now. Long, slow-rolling movement, with a bit of choppy pitch, still, but now it's more regular. Not too bad.

"I'd better fix that coolant leak," I tell Andrei.

"Yes. And then take your rest period. We're out of the turbulence now. I can handle it alone."

UNPLUG.

PLUG IN.

Didn't sleep too well. Dreamed about Marlene, just like she was still alive.

Ship's riding along easily now, inside the ocean, more like a submarine than a dirigible. Andrei's lolling in his couch. The scientists are happy as kids in a cave, with a whole new world to explore. Every instrument we've got is going full bore. Visions of Nobel Prizes floating out there.

Can't see much else. Really black now. Even the infrared's just about useless. It's sonar or nothing. No more snowflakes. Maybe they're still out there, but they don't register on the sonar.

"Did you have a good sleep?" Andrei asks.

"So-so. Kind of tense, excited. I feel more relaxed when I'm up here, plugged in. Got something to do, somebody to talk to. It's alone back there in the cocoon. Unplugged, unconnected. Nothing to do but think and worry."

Andrei says nothing. The connectors hide most of his face; all I can see is his mouth and chin. But I get the feeling that what I've said somehow disturbs him.

Bromley braced me back there. I was on my way back from the generator bay, heading for the cocoon. He floated out of his own compartment and blocked the passageway.

"Could we speak to you for a moment, in private?"

That's a laugh: in private.

"Who's we?" I asked him.

Bromley nodded toward Ludongo's cubby and drifted toward the hatch to it. I pushed a foot against the passageway bulkhead and followed him. Ludongo was sitting on his couch. His instruments were all on automatic, and he reached over to snap off his intercom screen when I hunched in. That's what they meant by private.

"We want to talk with you," he rumbled in his pressure-deepened bass.

"In strict confidence," Bromley added. "If you feel that you can't keep what we say confidential, then . . ." He let the idea dangle.

"I'll listen," I said. "If you're starting to say things I can't keep quiet about, I'll tell you."

"Fair enough," said Ludongo. He looked up at Bromley, who was bobbing nervously in front of the workbench.

"Em . . . we're worried about Captain Voronov," Bromley said.

"Worried about him?"

Ludongo said, "We don't like the arbitrary way he decided to plunge into the ocean. That was not only a dangerous decision, but an unfair one."

"Who's *we?*" I asked again.

"We scientists, of course," Bromley said.

"All four of you?"

"Speer feels exactly as we do. Ling is naturally more reticent about his feelings, but he's upset also."

I looked at Bromley. Inside that rubbery face

was a born troublemaker; the kind that starts fights and then stands off at the sidelines holding the coats and watching the blood flow.

"He's the captain," I said. "He had to make a fast decision. There wasn't any time for a conference or a vote."

Bromley countered. "There were a number of other things he could have done. He could have reversed our course, or gone up *over* the storm. . . ."

I shook my head. "Costs too much energy. He's got to consider the whole mission. You wouldn't want to get caught down here in a week or so without power, would you?"

"Of course not," said Ludongo. "Maybe the captain made the best decision. We're not arguing that point. It's merely the manner in which it was made. We should have been consulted."

"No time for it."

"Nonsense!" Bromley slashed. "It's his attitude, that's all. He's acting as if this is a warship, and we're nothing but crew members under his command."

"That's right. This *is* a military mission. That's why military men are in charge."

"You two are in charge," Bromley shook a finger at me stirring a tiny trail of bubbles, "because you're experienced in ship handling. The purpose of this mission is scientific. There isn't the faintest military reason for this expedition."

I felt myself starting to simmer. "Come on

now. If there weren't those damned machines on Titan we wouldn't be here, and you know it.''

"Yes,'' Ludongo answered, smiling a political smile, "that's true. But you don't actually expect to find the builders down here, do you?''

"You're the scientists. You tell me.''

"What makes you so certain that those buildings represent a military threat to man?'' Bromley asked.

How could he be so blind? "Any race that can set up machinery that runs unattended for God-only-knows how many centuries has a technology that's capable of crushing us. You know that!''

"But what makes you think they'd be hostile?''

"Why are the machines still running?''

With a look of disgust, Bromley told me, "The machines could be completely benign toward us. More likely, they're absolutely indifferent—their builders probably never gave a damn about us one way or the other.''

"I have my own idea,'' said Ludongo. "I have been on Mars. I have seen the artifacts there. They were created by human hands, built to human scale for human uses.''

"Yes, I know,'' Bromley muttered.

"There was a human civilization before the Ice Age. A civilization that reached Mars, perhaps even Titan. Those buildings and the machinery inside them could have been put up by our own ancestors.''

I asked, "What happened to that civilization?"

Shrugging, Ludongo answered, "War. Natural catastrophe."

"The Ice Age could have easily wiped it out," Bromley suggested.

"On Earth," I said. "What happened on Mars, on the Moon? And why are the buildings on Titan still standing? What are the machines doing?"

No answers.

"Okay, you could be right," I said. "Maybe there's nothing to be worried about. But there's still a good chance that the works on Titan were built by another race. We can't just assume they're friendly, or even neutral."

"They're probably dead and gone by now," Bromley said.

"At least they're gone," Ludongo added.

They still didn't get it. "Look. From a military point of view, we've got to assume that those buildings represent a possible threat. We've got to be ready for that threat. If it never materializes, fine. But if it does come and we're not ready for it . . . good-bye to the whole human race. For keeps!"

"How could you possibly expect to be ready. . . ."

"We've drifted away from the original subject," Ludongo said uneasily.

"No, this is exactly on the subject," I insisted. "This is a military mission. The captain's job is to seek out any alien life forms that we can find, and get enough data about them to decide whether or not they might have built the machines on Titan.''

"That's arrant nonsense! No creatures who live in this black gravity pit could even realize that there *are* other worlds, let alone build interplanetary ships!''

"Maybe so, but we're here to find out for sure. You scientists are supposed to provide the information. The captain and I are here to run the ship and see that the mission objectives are carried out.''

Bromley's face seemed to puff out even more with anger. He looked past me, to Ludongo. "I told you it'd do no good to talk to him. Bloody fools all think alike. Military mission!'' He turned on me. "You're here to ferry us about and see to it that we're safe and comfortable. This is a *scientific* expedition and there's not a damned jot of military necessity behind it . . . except what you gold-braided barbarians make up out of thin air!''

"Okay, that's enough," I snapped. "You can think whatever you like, but the truth is you're on a military ride and you'll take orders from the captain just like any crewman on a military ship. Period.''

I didn't wait for an answer. I pushed through the hatch and swam up the passageway to the flight deck.

Sitting here thinking about it, it's almost funny. Bromley's weird. He really thinks we'd be risking our butts in this soup just to give him a chance to satisfy his scientific curiosity.

SONAR CONTACT

Six faint white blips in the middle of the gray, grainy sonar view. Nothing else visible. Computer's flashing data: course, current vector, range, closing speed.

Andrei mumbles, "Fifty kilometers away and closing on us at better than fifty kilometers per hour."

"Look at that current vector. Unless the computer's blown a circuit, they're moving *against* the current."

Andrei goes to the intercom. "Sonar has detected six large objects approaching us. They are moving upstream, against the prevailing current."

Ling's the first one to answer. "Is this the maximum enlargement you can provide?" He's got the sonar display on his main screen.

"Yessir," I answer. "It's on max. When they get into closer range we can switch to other sensors."

Ludongo, "Can the computer make the size estimate?"

TWO POINT FIVE TO THREE POINT FIVE KILOMETERS PLUS OR MINUS TWENTY PERCENT.

Kilometers! Not a word from the scientists now. They're all watching the sonar display. Ling's trying to view them on infrared, as well. About all you can tell at the range is that they're slightly warmer than the sea itself.

They've disappeared!

"My screen's gone blank!"

"What happened?"

"Hold on, hold on," I yell at them. Check the screens. Get a wide-angle view. Yeah, there they are . . . look at 'em go!

"They're running away from us!"

"They sure are," I say.

Andrei's watching them dwindle in the distance on the wide-angle sonar view. "I thought we had lost them entirely when they jumped out of sight on the close-up. Give me a speed estimate."

ONE HUNDRED EIGHTY KILOMETERS PER HOUR PLUS OR MINUS FIVE PERCENT.

"I don't believe it," I mutter.

CONFIRMED.

"We certainly won't be able to catch up with them," Andrei says. Very practical thought.

"They *are* alive," Ling says, awed. Looking in on his compartment, I see that he's knocked the empty sonar display off his main screen and is rerunning the tape showing the animals.

"Alive," Speer echoes. "And so huge."

"Like whales," Andrei says. "Jovian whales. Have any of you hunted whales?"

No answers.

"Well, I have. When I was much younger. Whales can be very intelligent beasts . . . extremely intelligent."

Bromley chimes in, "Do they build machinery, Captain?"

"No. But they learn to run at the sight of danger. Those Jovian whales ran away from something. They sensed us, probably, and bolted. Why should they do that?"

I flick a peek at Andrei. His mouth's set in a tight line.

"Are you suggesting that these animals are accustomed to being hunted?" Bromley asks. His voice is dripping disbelief.

"They certainly acted frightened."

"Nonsense!" Bromley snorts.

Ludongo says, "But there's the infall of biological snow from the clouds above. This ocean is like a constantly replenished biological soup. . . ."

Bromley, "More like a biological vichyssoise, considering the temperatures out there."

"The point is," Ludongo resumes, "that the whales have a steady food supply. Why should there be predators when there's a plentiful supply of free food?"

I can sense Andrei shrugging. "Terrestrial baleen whales eat plankton . . . also free. Yet they are preyed upon by orcas, sharks—and submarines carrying men."

"You're not suggesting that these whales are hunted by intelligent creatures?" Bromley looks really upset. He doesn't want to believe a word of it, but his face shows absolute fear.

"I am suggesting only that those whales were frightened by us, and they couldn't be frightened unless they are accustomed to being hunted."

Ling gives a little cough. "Excuse my interruption, please. But it seems that these arguments cannot be resolved until we learn more about the creatures themselves. Can anyone suggest a technique by which we can study them at close range?"

"Not if they run when they see us," Bromley says.

Speer adds, "And they detected us at fifty kilometers, didn't they?"

"Then how can we get close to them?" Ludongo asks.

Andrei knows, I'm sure. But he's hesitating. Probably used the technique hunting whales in the Antarctic. Russian subs have done it to our patrols. And vice versa. They're supposed to work together on whaling hunts, but sometimes they play games. What the hell, I'll break the ice.

"We can try to spoof the whales' sonar," I tell them.

"What's that?"

I peek at Andrei again. He's broken into a broad grin.

"Check the sonar tapes," I say, "to find the frequency that the whales used to detect us. Then amplify our return signal on that same frequency. It'll make the whales think we're one of them. Instead of running, they might let us get close."

"Exactly," Andrei agrees. "The trick works against terrestrial whales. . . . Even against other submarine crews, when you're trying to lead them away from the real whales."

We laugh together. For once everybody's in agreement. The computer has a record of the sonar frequency the whales put out. It's lower than anything we can do. So Andrei goes aft to jury-rig one of the transmitters so it'll match the whales' frequency.

Alone now. Ship's completely mine again. Feels good. Nothing around us. Riding smooth and easy.

Funny I dreamed about Marlene. Haven't thought about her since the accident. Maybe it wasn't a dream. Too logical. Maybe I just remembered about her while I tried to sleep.

THERE IS NO RECORD OF YOUR DREAM IN THE SHIP'S LOG.

Damned right there isn't.

MISSION OBJECTIVE FOURTEEN REQUIRES THAT PSYCHOLOGICAL RECORDS BE MAINTAINED AS FULLY AS POSSIBLE.

I know. They want to study our dreams. They claim it's important for the next mission. Especially if we don't make it back. Get it into the recorder so they'll be able to figure out if we went off the deep end.

VOCALIZATION OF SUBCONSCIOUS ACTIVITIES SUCH AS DREAMS IS HELD IN STRICT PRIVACY.

Sure. Only two or three dozen psychs will hear me spill my guts. Okay, can't argue with mission objective fourteen. I'll try to remember the dream. For the psychs. For the next set of poor bastards they send in here.

It was the time we jetted over to the sequoia forest. After a couple of months on that flat Texas scrubland, we wanted to see mountains and real trees again. Not the transplants at the Training Center.

The park was filled with tourists, even a plane load of Scouts from Indonesia. We ducked off the main trail and climbed up away from them. The trees are as big and tall as rocket boosters; been standing there for two thousand years. And those damned people crawling around clicking cameras, yelling after kids, carving initials. Sacrilegious.

"Look at 'em," I said to Marlene when we stopped for breath halfway up the slope. "Not a care in the world. This damned Titan business doesn't mean a thing to them."

She answered, "Perhaps they're trying very hard to forget about Titan."

She was inclined to be serious: a Germanic trait, I guess. She'd already told me several times that she wasn't going to fall in love with me because the chances were that we'd be sent on different missions, and besides she was older than I.

We worked our way deeper into the forest, hiking up the slope, away from the noise of the tourists. We both had backpacks; plenty of food. The big trees made a canopy of cool shade far overhead, but every once in a while a shaft of sunlight would break through and set off highlights in Marlene's hair.

"Actually," she said thoughtfully, "life has become much better since the discovery of the buildings on Titan. All the international tensions that our fathers worried about have dried up. The idea of a war between nations seems ridiculous now."

I laughed. "Sure. Why worry about blowing each other to hell when there's a race somewhere that can do it for us?"

"But it's much more distant a threat, a remote possibility. That race visited the solar system thousands of years ago. Perhaps thousands of centuries ago. They may never come back."

"Then why are the machines still working?" I asked. "And what are they doing?"

"That *is* the disquieting part of it," she admitted.

We found a flat stretch near a cold stream. We could hear birds now, and a squirrel jabbered at us from the base of a burnt-out tree. I unslung the pack from my shoulders and we had lunch.

Later on, when we were stretched out side by side, I asked her, "You were there. What's it really like?"

She was staring up into the trees. "It's . . . very hard to describe. Not the physical conditions; you've seen tapes on the buildings and you know what Titan's like. . . ."

"Pretty damned dark and gloomy, except when Saturn's up."

"You forget Saturn's in the sky," Marlene said. "You can . . . *feel* the machinery throbbing. The ground vibrates. When you're near the buildings, the sensation you get . . . it makes your flesh crawl."

"They ought to hit it with a nuke missile and make everybody feel better."

"But suppose the machines are sending out a signal? Some wave length that we can't detect? If we stop that signal, it would tell those who built the machines that it's time to return to the solar system." Her eyes were wide now with real fear.

I had run out of flip answers.

"I spent three years there," she was quieter now, "and we knew just as much about the machines when I left as when I had arrived. We don't dare dismantle them. I'm not even sure that we could if we tried."

I lay back and watched the swaying green canopy was above us. Fresh and alive and good. "Must be like living next to a haunted house."

"That's exactly it."

I put my arm around her shoulders. Instead of drawing closer to me, though, she said:

"Bob, when I was on Titan . . ."

"I don't want to talk about Titan or anything else."

"No . . . I've got to tell you."

"Marlene, you don't have to. . . ."

"Yes, I do," she said. She sat up, then turned to look back at me. "I saw a man try to kill himself on Titan. He just walked off into the sea one day. We barely got to him in time. He was unlocking his helmet when we reached him."

I must have shrugged.

"You see . . . I was in love with him. He was married, but his wife had stayed on Earth, and we . . ." Her voice trailed off.

"But I thought you and I . . . we've got something good going between us, Marlene."

"I know. Honestly, I thought I had forgotten him, that what happened on Titan was all over . . . but yesterday I saw him again. He's at the Training Center now, trying to qualify for a star mission."

"And you still love him?"

There was pain in her eyes. "Bob, I don't know. Until yesterday you were the only man I cared about. But now—he didn't even see me, I only caught a glimpse of him as he got off the shuttle. . . ."

"Maybe you were mistaken. Maybe it isn't him."

"No, I checked. It's him. He's been in the hospital for more than a year, but now he's at the Training Center. It's him."

Great, I thought. *So we'll have a triangle heading out for the stars. Maybe we can all get freezer beds next to each other.*

That was before I knew I'd be sent to Jupiter, not on a star mission. And before she died.

Andrei's back. Checking the sonar transmitter, matching its output against the computer memory of the whales' frequency. Flash me a comparison. Looks good. Check sonar. Nothing out there now, sea's empty.

Controls feel sluggish. Nothing definite, no alarms. Just not responding as smoothly as they should. Maybe it's the outside pressure. Up to seventy tons per square centimeter.

Andrei's not plugged in yet, still playing with the sonar.

"Looks good to me," I tell him.

He nods. But he looks sort of grim, preoccupied. "Yes, I suppose it will do." He hesitates. Then, "Can you handle the controls by yourself for a while longer? I want to check something with Speer."

"You feel sick?"

"I'm having a little trouble breathing."

I look at him. He means it. "But you're not breathing. The gills are."

Frowning, "Yes, of course. I mean I'm having some soreness in my chest. Perhaps I'm merely tired."

"Well, you'd better check it out."

He puts his hand on my shoulder. "Don't be worried. It's nothing serious, I'm sure. Speer will probably say it's psychological. . . . You know, I really don't enjoy being plugged into the ship. It bothers me. It makes me feel less than human."

"Less? I get just the opposite feeling."

He bangs my shoulder. "Good. I'll let Speer poke at me and then take my rest period. Call me if anything unusual develops."

That's almost funny. "How do you define unusual?"

He laughed. "Use your judgment, comrade."

Alone again. Odd that Andrei should feel that way. Being plugged in . . . it's beyond being human. Can think with the speed of light, see what no human could ever see for himself, swim the depths of Jupiter's seas. All human frailties and fears wiped out, buried, forgotten.

SYSTEM ANOMALY REPORT.

Go ahead.

PRESSURE TRANSDUCERS ON MAIN HULL SHOW LOCAL INCREASE OF EXTERIOR PRESSURE ON PORT QUARTER OF NOSE SECTION. INTERIOR PRESSURE BETWEEN MAIN AND SECONDARY HULLS HAS BEEN INCREASED AUTOMATICALLY TO COMPENSATE.

Display data.

Curves don't look too bad. All parameters within

tolerable limits. Check possible reasons for pressure rise and display most likely.

LOGIC WORKING. MOST LIKELY CAUSE IS HULL CORROSION LEADING TO WEAKENING OF MAIN HULL STRUCTURAL STRENGTH. SECOND MOST LIKELY CAUSE IS TRANSDUCER FAILURE. AUTO-CHECK SHOWS TRANSDUCER OPERATING NORMALLY.

Hull corrosion. That could lead to major failure.

ALL PARAMETERS WITHIN TOLERABLE LIMITS.

At present. Display projected estimate of hull integrity over next twenty-four hours.

INSUFFICIENT DATA FOR PROJECTION.

Understood. Monitor hull pressure continuously. Flash yellow alert when structural integrity drops five percent from current value.

THAT WILL STILL BE WITHIN TOLERABLE LIMITS.

Understood. Execute order as given.

UNDERSTOOD.

And also review all mission objectives by priority rating. List all priority objectives that can be accomplished in periods of twelve, twenty-four, thirty-six, and forty-eight hours.

UNDERSTOOD. WORKING.

And maintain continuous watch on hull pressure.

EXECUTING AS PREVIOUSLY ORDERED. . . . SONAR CONTACT.

Display. Yes, there they are. Ten . . . fifteen
. . . seventeen of them. Range?

SIXTY-THREE KILOMETERS.

Display their course and relative velocity. Estimate time to intercept.

TWO HOURS TEN MINUTES PLUS OR
MINUS FIVE PERCENT.

Execute intercept course. Any change in hull
pressure?

ALL PARAMETERS WITHIN TOLERABLE
LIMITS.

"Seventeen big ones on sonar," I sing out on
the intercom. "If they've detected us at all, our
sonar spoofing has fooled them. So far."

The scientists must have been sleeping. Takes
them a few minutes to get started again. Now I can
see that they've all got the sonar display on their
screens. Andrei's in the cocoon; leave him there.
Nothing will happen for two hours or more.

Sonar view again. "We don't know how sensitive their accoustical gear is," I tell the scientists.
"We're matching their own outputs as closely as
possible. Our engine noise is muffled as much as
we can. We should run silent, in case they're
sensitive to other frequencies. Don't make unneces-
sary noise."

It's easy to keep quiet. The whales are just too
awesome for words. Even in the gray, ghostly
sonar view they look tremendous, gliding effort-

lessly through the ocean in a loose herd. We're gaining on them slowly, holding our breaths.

Can't see much detail about them with sonar. But they're slowly getting bigger and bigger. It's like driving toward the mountains from the flatlands. You think you're close, but they just keep looming higher and wider and grander all the time. Sonar's getting jumbled now, too many echoes bouncing around. Display's starting to look like a badly tuned video picture. Switch to infrared.

Better. They radiate nicely. Look slightly orange. They've got tail flukes something like a whale's; maybe smaller in proportion to the body. And a fin or something under the gut. Edge closer to them, careful, don't make any sudden moves, nothing that will scare them.

Hard to tell their real size, nothing to compare them against. Give me a rundown on the numbers you've got.

AVERAGE LENGTH: TWO POINT EIGHT KILOMETERS. MAXIMUM LENGTH: THREE POINT SEVEN KILOMETERS. MINIMUM LENGTH: TWO POINT ONE FIVE KILOMETERS. DENSITY UNKNOWN. MASS UNKNOWN.

Pulling up astern of them now. Feel like a flea trailing a parade of elephants. It'd take ten minutes to travel the length of one of them with our engines on max standard power. God, it's been two hours since we first sighted them!

Andrei slips quietly into his couch.

"Want the controls?" I whisper, glancing at him with the intercom eyes.

He shakes his head. "No, you're doing very well." He pulls the sensor unit up in front of his eyes, but doesn't touch any of the controls or communications connectors.

Ling pipes up, "Can we pull closer to them?"

"Don't go between them," Andrei orders.

"Are we close enough to use video?" Ludongo asks.

"What do you think?" I ask Andrei.

"I doubt that they're sensitive to light," he says. "Try a few short bursts with the laser first, to see if there is any reaction.

I steer out alongside the herd, then settle as close as I dare to one of the outer bulls. Not that I can tell a damned thing about their sex, if they have any. But the outermost whales are the biggest. Laser beam doesn't seem to bother him. Put it on fast scan and hook in the video. Back away so we can get the whole animal on the viewscreen.

Listen to them gasp!

Now we can see them for real, in color and all. They're staggering. Built more like an armless squid than anything else. Flukes in the tail, but they seem to be more for maintaining trim than for propulsion.

Mammoth open mouth up front; maybe it's permanently open. Can't see any teeth. There's a siphon under the belly pulsing rhythmically. No wonder they can dash so fast; they're jet-propelled. No eyes, no fins except the tail flukes. Sleek and streamlined. Powerful. Glossy gray-green color. Mouth's big enough to swallow a town. If they had teeth, we'd be a toothpick size for them. Pretty thought!

Nobody's saying a word now. I could watch these giants all day. They're just gliding along in formation, outer bulls weaving back and forth a little. Can't make out any real small members inside the pack, but there's a pretty tight knot of cows in the center. Maybe they're protecting the youngsters.

From what?

Every instrument on the ship's grinding away; power drain's at max. Just keeping up with these whales while they're grazing is straining the engines.

"Is there any way we can get samples of their tissue?" Ling asks. I hope it's rhetorical.

Bromley says, "I suppose we could slice off a bit with the high-power laser."

I glance at Andrei.

He reaches for the intercom unit. "Our orders are to conduct remote observations of any life forms discovered. No direct contact unless it is forced upon us. No samples, I'm sorry."

"Oh, come now," Bromley argues. "A little nick off one of those flukes . . ."

"We have no way of knowing how the animal would react," Andrei says. "I wouldn't want to be close to one when it started thrashing around, would you?"

No answer. Discussion ended.

"How're you feeling?" I ask him.

"Not too bad. Speer says he can't find anything physically wrong."

"Want to rest some more?"

"No. . . . It's time for your rest period, isn't it?"

"I'm not tired."

"Never mind. Go back and sleep."

It's funny. He sounds so reluctant. He doesn't want to plug in. And he doesn't realize how much I don't want to unplug.

"Something you ought to know." I tell him about the hull, show him the computer's estimates, and then flash the priority lists.

"I haven't told the scientists about it yet, and observing the whales overrides all the other priority mission objectives. Looks like the pressure's holding steady, even though it's a little high. Probably the hull will be okay as long as we don't go any deeper."

Andrei still hasn't plugged in. I can see his whole face. He looks positively happy.

"I understand. We will start the twelve-hour priority list and do as much as we can. If the hull still is good after that, we will stretch it for another twelve hours. But that's all. After that we go up."

"What do you think the scientists are going to say?"

He shrugs. "That is irrelevant."

Fine by me. Let him argue with them. Andrei slowly plugs himself in and takes over the control of the ship. It's time for me to go.

UNPLUG.

PLUG IN.

Pain! Lights flashing, ship tumbling wildly.

"What's the matter? What's going on?"

I'm slapping on connectors as fast as I can. Ship's lurching like a runaway drunk. Andrei looks bad.

"Can't . . . control . . . can't . . ."

"Speer! Get up here fast!" Check all systems. Give me just the emergency data.

STABILIZER OVERLOADED. MANUAL OVERRIDE REQUIRED.

I'm trying, I'm trying! Outside view. Nothing. Where'd the whales go?

"Speer! Where the hell are you?"

"I'm right here!" he screams through my earphone from a few centimeters away.

Inside view. Speer's unplugging Andrei. Captain's arms are floating limply, head lolling back, mouth sagging open. Ship still buffeting. Fighting for control. Stabilizer coming around . . . slewing and rolling. . . .

"What the hell happened? I was in the cocoon when everything seemed to bust loose."

"I don't know," Speer shouts. "It all happened so fast. The captain yelled something and the ship seemed to roll completely over. Lights went off for a moment. I fell out of my couch. . . . I think Dr. Ling's been hurt."

Got her righted now. Bouncing's smoothed out. Stabilizer starting to respond on its own. Any red alerts?

NO RED ALERTS. ALL SYSTEMS FUNCTIONING WITHIN TOLERABLE LIMITS.

Speer's still struggling with the captain.

"Ludongo, Bromley . . . one of you get up here and give Speer a hand."

We're all in one piece. Run a complete systems check, display anything outside nominal values. Display hull pressure.

ONE PERCENT INCREASE IN PRESSURE AT PORT NOSE SECTION. STILL WITHIN TOLERABLE LIMITS. ALL OTHER SYSTEMS FUNCTIONING AT NORMAL VALUES.

Okay. Rerun the sensor tapes for the past ten minutes so I can figure out what happened.

Video view, good. There are the whales, still feeding. Everything peaceful enough . . . what are those? Different . . . look at the whales buck! There they go, top speed, right out of sight. Wide-angle sonar view now . . . more animals zooming in. Not whales, though. Too small. Different shape.

Delta form, faster, tighter formation. Look like manta rays or sharks. Zooming in like rocket planes . . . hey, they're coming right at us!

Blackout.

Back to real time. Outside view. Still nothing. Whatever they were, they're gone.

Intercom. Speer's got Andrei on the emergency couch in medical bay, next to his own compartment. With these damned gills, you can't tell if a man's breathing or not. Close-up. Yep, the gills are pulsing. But damned slow. And why'd they have to make them green?

"Speer, how's he doing?"

"I . . . I don't know," Speer says, looking miserable. "He has some of the symptoms of shock. Blood pressure's very low. I'm going to try pressure cuffs to pump the blood back up from his legs and lower torso."

"Dr. Ling needs help also," Ludongo says.

Look in on Ling's compartment. He's got a gash on his forehead. Blood seeping out making a reddish cloud that drifts in the circulation currents up toward the exhaust duct in the overhead. Ludongo's in there with him.

"It's not a serious wound," Ling says calmly. "Attend to the captain first."

"Somebody put a patch on him, at least," I say.

Ludongo looks up at the intercom screen. Bromley, back in his own cubicle, says, "I'll get a first-aid kit."

Okay. They're helping each other. Ship's handling all right now. Controls still sluggish, though. Stabilizer acting okay. Andrei must've turned off our fake-whale signal. Why?

"Does anyone understand what happened to us?" Ludongo asks. He's sitting alongside Ling, who now has a white plastic gummed onto his brown skin from one nonexistent eyebrow halfway back to the top of his skull. It's about three times more bandage than the cut needed, but at least the bleeding's stopped.

"We were attacked by the sharks, or whatever they were," I tell them.

Ling agrees. "I was watching the viewscreen when it happened. The new type of creature is clearly a predator."

"Sharks," Bromley mutters.

"And we outsmarted ourselves," I realize. "Our sonar trick fooled the sharks. They thought we were a whale. When the real whales took off and we just stood here, they jumped us."

"But how?" Ludongo asks. "Did they ram the ship? What did they do to us?"

Good questions. We rerun the tapes. Four times. In ultra-slow motion. The computer checks their sizes, speeds, closing rates. Up at the front end of their manta-shaped bodies is a snout that may or may not have a mouth in it. They're about a quarter the size of the whales—still more than ten times our size. And the computer is very definite that the nearest shark was still half a kilommeter away from us when Andrei shouted and the ship went haywire.

Now we're all silent. Very, very silent. Speer standing over the captain, Ling on his couch with the other two beside him, and me up in the flight deck.

The sharks have something that can knock this ship for a loop. Something that acts over a range of half a kilometer. A weapon.

"You're not suggesting that they're actually intelligent?" Bromley asks finally, his voice strained.

"Who can say?" Ludongo replies. "Are dolphins intelligent?"

"We must learn more about them," Ling says.

"But how?"

"Decoy them again," I answer. "Put on our whale camouflage and wait for them to find us."

"We can't risk it!" says Speer. "The captain's been hurt. What happens if you . . ." His voice fades out.

Bromley chips in. "Yes, and how long can you stay at the controls of this ship without collapsing from fatigue? I vote that we get out while we're still able to. We've already discovered much more than anyone expected us to."

"Still," Ling says, "it would be extremely valuable to study these creatures further. If they are intelligent . . ."

I tell them, "Discovery of an intelligent creature falls under the primary mission objective. The most important task we have is to determine if the sharks are intelligent or not."

"Wait," Bromley says. "What about the hull? The captain told us that the hull is showing signs of corrosion and we must pull out in twelve hours. So any further arguments are purely academic."

"We still have twelve hours to see what we can accomplish," I say. "And longer, if we need it. The primary mission objective takes precedence over all other considerations, including the personal safety of the crew."

"What? That's absolute madness!"

"What about the captain?" Speer bleats. "We should be getting him to proper medical treatment."

"Will twelve hours be critical?" I ask.

"Of course! Twelve minutes might be critical. I can't really diagnose him accurately here. . . ."

What would Andrei do if I was stretched out on the sick bay couch? Twelve hours. He's in shock. If he's lived through the first few minutes he ought to be okay. Speer can take care of him. Ship's all mine now, my decision to make. Another twelve hours. All mine for another twelve hours. Maybe longer.

"We'll stay," I tell them. "Speer, let me know if he gets any worse. We'll put out the whale sonar signal. If the sharks show up, we'll try some long-range looks at them and then turn off the whale signal.''

"If they have any intelligence at all," Bromley says, "the sonar camouflage won't fool them. They'll know we're not a whale.''

"It fooled them once.''

"Did it?"

Hadn't thought of that. Ignore it. "Okay. The computer will give each of you a priority list of measurements that must be made. Carry out as many as you can, starting at the top of the list. If and when we make contact with alien life forms, all instruments will be devoted to getting as much data on them as possible.''

Bromley mutters, "Another ruddy admiral handing down orders to his deck hands.''

But they're getting to work. Keep them busy. Suppose the sharks are intelligent? Suppose they're the ones who built the machines on Titan? What kind of weapon did they use on the ship? What else do they have?

LOG REQUIRES REPORT ON YOUR SUB-CONSCIOUS ACTIVITY DURING YOUR SLEEP PERIOD.

Not now, I'm busy.

REVISED MISSION SCHEDULE INDICATES LACK OF FIRST PRIORITY OBJECTIVES AT PRESENT. SUBCONSCIOUS ACTIVITY RE-PORT CAN BE FILED NOW.

I didn't really dream. . . .

EYE MOVEMENT MONITOR AND EEG TAPE
SHOW EVIDENCE OF SUBCONSCIOUS AC-
TIVITY DURING SLEEP PERIOD. MISSION OB-
JECTIVE FOURTEEN . . .

Okay, okay . . . but it wasn't much of anything.
It was kind of mixed up, weird. Part of it was the
last time I saw Marlene.

I had been fitted out with the gills. They had us
living in test tanks. The tanks connected with the
lake and we could spend our free time there if we
felt like it. I had been there for an hour or so,
watching the dolphins they had stocked the lake
with. To keep us company.

Marlene hadn't told me she was coming to see
me. She just showed up with a tank strapped to her
back and her face covered by a goggled mask. But
I recognized her immediately. Even with her hair
pulled back I knew her the instant I saw her.

"They've taken all your hair off," was the first
thing she said, from inside the mask.

"More than you know," I answered. I was
wearing trunks.

We swam for a long time, hooked rides on the
dolphins, talked about trivialities, hardly touched
each other.

"I've got my assignment," she said at last.
"Sirius."

"Same as your friend?"

"Yes."

"Was it a tough job to wangle the same mission? Did you have to lay any of the administrators or personnel people?"

"Bob, don't be . . ."

"Don't be what?" I asked.

And somehow it was a different time and place. I was sitting in front of a desk while a fat civilian was telling me:

"Don't be disappointed that you weren't accepted for a star mission. Only a handful of the very finest scientists and astronauts could be picked. There's an even more challenging assignment waiting for you, if you're willing to tackle it."

I must have asked him what it was.

"Jupiter. Far more dangerous and hostile than any star mission. The most difficult challenge we have ever faced. And probably the most important. Certainly the most rigorous mission we've attempted so far."

Note the *we*. He never got closer to Jupiter than the men's room down the hall from his office.

But then the dream changed again. I was standing alone, watching while Marlene died. It was confused, mixed up. The noise was shattering. Flames and smoke, people shouting and pointing . . .

CAN YOU DESCRIBE THE SCENE MORE CLEARLY?

No, it's all a jumble.

CONTINUE.

That's all there is. End of dream. End of report.

Give me a sonar sweep, max range. Still nothing. Okay, systems check. Controls still heavy. Don't like the way the stabilizer . . . hey, why are we nose-down?

SHIP'S ATTITUDE IS SET AT ONE POINT FIVE DEGREES DESCENT.

The hell it is. I want her straight and level. Maintain constant depth.

STABILIZER OVERRIDE REQUIRED.

Override it, then. Keep us straight and level. Check ship's attitude every five minutes. If the stabilizer can't keep us level, override it.

UNDERSTOOD.

"Speer, how's the captain?"

Young as he is, Speer's squinting nearsightedly at the sick bay instrument board. "His condition is about the same. Comatose. Blood pressure low but steady."

"Will he make it?"

He shrugs elaborately. "If we were on Earth, or even on one of the orbiting ships . . ."

He's looking for a bowl of water to wash away his responsibility.

"Are you still insisting on this madness?" Bromley's whine. "We haven't found any more animals. Give it up, and for God's sake, let's get out of here while we still can."

Hull pressure report.

NO RISE IN PRESSURE SINCE LAST REPORT.

Minimum time to failure?

INSUFFICIENT DATA.

"All systems are within tolerable limits," I say into the intercom. "We will continue the mission."

Dr. Ling, sounding a little weaker than before, says, "I wish to go on record as requesting that we remain at least long enough to make another attempt at observing the native life forms. If possible, I would like to sample some tissue."

Tough old bird; he'd probably go after Jovian whale hide with his teeth if he had to.

"Dr. Ludongo, do you wish to make any comment for the ship's log?"

After a moment's hesitation he answers, "I am concerned about the captain's health and the ship's safety. However, I realize the importance of our mission and wish to continue . . . unless the risks become too great."

Hah! His father couldn't have straddled the fence any better.

SONAR CONTACT.

Display it. Six blips. Too far out to tell what they are. Keep them in sight. Follow them. Display size estimates as soon as sufficient data is recorded.

OVERRIDING STABILIZER TO MAINTAIN LEVEL ATTITUDE.

Understood.

"We have six objects on sonar," I tell them, punching the sonar display onto their screens.

"Are they whales or sharks?" Ludongo asks.

"Probably whales. They're cruising peacefully. Too far off to sense us."

Bromley says, "If they're sharks and they attack us . . ."

"Computer is pre-set to turn off our whale signal if sonar return shows they're sharks."

Bromley doesn't look happy at all; I can see him shudder.

AT PRESENT HEADING AND SPEED INTERCEPTION OF SONAR CONTACT WILL BE IN ONE HOUR TWENTY-FIVE MINUTES PLUS OR MINUS TEN PERCENT. MISSION PROFILE CALLS FOR CO-PILOT REST PERIOD AT THIS TIME.

Can't rest. Captain's in sick bay.

EMERGENCY PROCEDURE CALLS FOR CO-PILOT TO RECEIVE NUTRIENTS AND DISCONNECT FROM ACTIVE SHIP CONTROL WHILE MAINTAINING NEURAL CONNECTIONS WITH COMPUTER AND SENSORS.

Watching myself on the inside camera, I pull my hands and feet out of the control connectors. Now I reach between Andrei's couch and mine for the nutrient tube and plug it into the socket on my left arm. Andrei's is on his right arm. He used to joke that this was the way you could tell the captain from the co-pilot.

OVERRIDING STABILIZER.

I crank the couch back slightly and try to relax.

Sonar still shows six gray smudges. Guess I'm supposed to nap, but I don't want to. Dream too much. Like the time just before we boosted to orbit, when I was swimming in the lake and saw Marlene. She'd been dead for more than a month, but there she was swimming toward me. My heart just stopped. Only it wasn't her. When the girl got close enough I could see she didn't look anything like her. I don't want to dream about her now. Concentrate on the mission. Don't sleep. Don't dream.

OVERRIDING STABILIZER.

Must have dozed off after all. Computer turned off the sensor display.

Outside view. They're whales all right. More than six . . . two smaller ones in sight. Youngsters? Can't be sharks, they're riding right alongside one of the big ones.

Maintain max magnification and display all data as it comes in. Also maintain max warning range for any other contacts. Interrupt all displays if another contact appears.

UNDERSTOOD.

Look in on the scientists. They're resting now, letting the instruments pull in the data and record it. Ling's watching the sonar display while lying down. Bromley and Ludongo are chatting about something over the intercom. Science stuff. Speer's back in his own cubby, sleeping. Check on the captain. Still unconscious, looks like. Tap into the medical recorders. All displays fairly constant: heart rate, breathing, body temp. Holding his own, I guess.

NEW CONTACT.

Track it.

It's more than one. A dozen objects, whistling along in close formation out at the edge of our sonar range. They're on the far side of the whale pack. Probably they haven't picked us up at all.

They're sharks, no doubt about it. Can't tell their sizes or shapes at this distance, but just watching them move, you can see they're completely different from the whales. They're hunters. Killers.

"Sonar contact. Twelve sharks," I say on the intercom.

The scientists snap to life, stare at the sonar display.

"Observe max safety procedures," I tell them. They're already strapping in.

Range to whales?

FORTY-FIVE MINUTES TO INTERCEPTION.

Maintain constant distance from them. Follow them without getting any closer.

UNDERSTOOD.

So far the whales haven't detected the sharks at all. They're just lumbering along. The sharks are still out at the edge of our detection range. But now they're splitting up into smaller groups . . . two or three each.

"My God, they're going to surround the whales!" Bromley's voice, awe-stricken.

"Rather intelligent behavior," Ling says softly.

Ludongo, "Many predators on Earth are equally intelligent. The lion, for instance. And the wolf."

Two of the sharks are circling around behind the whales, while the rest are deploying themselves ahead of the herd and along the flanks. The whales still haven't noticed them.

Speer says, "They're going to be butchered. . . ."

TWO CONTACTS APPROACHING FORTY-FIVE-MINUTE RANGE.

"Shouldn't you be turning off the whale signal?" Bromley says.

Ludongo says, "If we turn off the signal the real whales might sense us and bolt."

"That could save their lives," says Ling. "Surely many of them will be killed if they don't begin to run soon."

"Mission objectives clearly state we are not to interfere with local ecological patterns," I remind them. "However, ship safety requirements have the highest priority."

OVERRIDING STABILIZER.

Understood. Will assume stabilizer override every five minutes until you report otherwise. No further need for override reports.

UNDERSTOOD.

Turn off the sonar signal. If the scientists could hold their breaths with the artificial gills, they'd be

doing it now. Nothing. The whales don't sense us.
And the two closest sharks are paying no attention
to us, either. They're lining up; the other sharks
are deployed in ambush.

There they go! Wide-angle view, follow them
in. The whales finally sense them. Look at them
buck! The whales are faster than the sharks . . . at
least for short sprints. They're going to bull right
past the sharks and break free.

God Almighty! Lightning bolts! Electric blasts
arcing from the sharks to the whales. Blank out
eyes when they flash. They're paralyzing the whales
with electricity.

"Stop them! Kill them!" Bromley's shouting.
"Don't let them do it! Use the laser on the sharks!"

The sharks are doing a thorough job. Electric
bolts stun the whales, then they latch on with their
snouts, like lamprey eels. Looks like they suck the
juices from the whales instead of eating the meat.
Most of the whales have two or three sharks attached to them now, drifting slowly, sinking.

One of the youngsters has managed to keep
clear of them. Heading our way, emitting all sorts
of high-pitched peeps. Three sharks closing in on
him.

"Save him!" Bromley shrieks. "Don't let them
get him!"

"Our mission is to observe, not interfere."

This time it happens no farther than ten kilometers from us. Infrared picks up good detail.

The little whale isn't much bigger than this ship.
He's fast, but the sharks have an angle on him.
Closing fast. Youngster's screeching louder and
louder. Or maybe it's just the Doppler effect. There
goes the lightning! Was that Bromley groaning?
Eyes recovered now. Whale's dead in the water.
One shark already stuck into him, other two move
in and hook on. It *is* obscene-looking.

Ludongo says, "Now we know how they attacked us. An electric arc . . . it makes an effec-
tive weapon."

"But a completely natural one," Ling says,
sounding tired, subdued. "They apparently have
no artifacts."

"The captain must've been jolted when their
electric arcs hit the ship. Doubt that he got an
electric shock—systems are protected against that.
But having several bolts slam into the ship and
overpower all the controls and sensors must've
been enough to send him into . . . what do you
call it, Speer?"

"Physiological shock."

"Yes. That help you? Can you treat him better
now?"

"Not really." He sounds sullen. Outside view
shows the baby whale and its three leeches drifting
just below us now.

"Why'd you have to let them get the little
one?" Speer asks.

I flick a look at him; he's practically in tears.

Bromley's livid. Hard to tell what Ludongo's expression means. Ling's impassive, but very quiet now. Sheer emotionalism. The whale was panicked and running blind. It wasn't heading for us deliberately. It couldn't know that we might have helped it.

Ling speaks up. "It seems there is a considerable amount of Jovian tissue nearby. Will it be possible to sample it?"

Looking out again, I see that the sharks have detached from the baby whale. It's still close to us, but starting to sink faster. The sharks have gone; there are no living creatures left nearby.

Nose ship down. Plot fastest intercept course.

WORKING. SYSTEMS CHECK SHOWS ALL SYSTEMS OPERATING WITHIN TOLERABLE LIMITS EXCEPT STABILIZER WHICH IS STILL BEING OVERRIDEN AT FIVE-MINUTE INTERVALS. PRESSURE IN NOSE SECTION MAY BECOME CRITICAL IF DEEP DIVE IS NECESSARY.

How deep?

INSUFFICIENT DATA.

Display any changes in nose pressure immediately.

UNDERSTOOD.

Ling uses the high-powered laser to vaporize some of the whale's flesh. Studies the light on spectrophotometer. Ludongo helps by probing the animal with high-frequency sonar to get some idea of density. Bromley tries neutron beam probe, but returns are too weak to be intelligible. Either not much solid structure inside the baby or Bromley's still too upset to work his instruments.

"Speer, how's the captain?"

He looks up from sick bay couch. "Worse. His breathing rate is slower. I think the higher pressure down at this depth is bothering him."

Check internal monitor. "But the internal pressure's only increased one point one percent."

"I don't care what the numbers are," he says angrily. "His gill rate is getting critical. It's getting hard for me to breathe, too. My gill rate's slowed down; I've checked it."

Pressure shouldn't bother them. Check performance ratings for gill systems. Curve shows pressure versus oxygen production. Now superimpose ship's current internal pressure readings. Pressure is approaching critical point, but not there yet.

Whale's still sinking.

"Dr. Ling, we will exceed safety margins if we go deeper."

"Do you have all the data you need?" Ludongo asks.

Ling smiles into the camera. "It would take several generations to get all the data that we need. But I have accomplished far more than I expected to. I can stop now, if you wish."

Good. Set course for surface and execute.

STABILIZER DOES NOT RESPOND.

Clarify that.

STABILIZER DOES NOT RESPOND TO CON-
TROL INPUT OR TO OVERRIDE. LOCKED IN
ONE DEGREE NOSE-DOWN POSITION. SUG-
GEST YOU ATTEMPT MANUAL OVERRIDE.

Useless. Track down the malfunction. Fast.

WORKING.

Possible causes of stabilizer failure: electrical,
hydraulic, mechanical. If electrical, can use alter-
nate circuit. If hydraulic, back-up system should
work. But if external pressure has overloaded the
system . . . and ship's nosing still deeper . . .

Flick on intercom. "Gentlemen, the stabilizer
system is temporarily inoperative."

Explaining it to them, watch their faces. Each
man in his own compartment. Each one showing
fear.

"Isn't there anything you can do?" Bromley
asks.

"Computer is working on the problem."

"You could use the engine thrust to push us up
out of this depth," Ludongo says. "Perhaps at
lighter pressures the stabilizer will work again."
He's running his hands along the edge of the
couch as he speaks.

"That might be tried if nothing else works."

"Why not now?" Speer asks.

"It would take an excessive amount of propulsion power to lift the ship while the stabilizer is
pointing nose-down. There might not be enough

power left to lift out of the atmosphere and return to orbit.''

''There is nothing for us to do but wait?'' asks Ling.

''That is right.''

''Tell me,'' Bromley says, his voice calm except for a slight tremor. ''How long can we remain in this nose-down attitude before we reach a depth that will crush the ship?''

''Insufficient data.''

They lapse into silence. Ludongo turns back to his workbench. Bromley leans back on his couch. Ling is rerunning data tapes. Speer fidgets around the captain.

Computer: Make a straight-line extrapolation of pressure gradient recorded so far, compare it to hull structural integrity, and display an estimated time to hull rupture. Private display circuit for flight deck only.

WORKING. AT PRESENT DESCENT RATE HULL RUPTURE WILL OCCUR IN TWO HOURS PLUS OR MINUS TWENTY PERCENT.

What about malfunction check on stabilizer?

NO MALFUNCTION ESTABLISHED. CIRCUITS OPERATING NORMALLY. SERVOS FUNCTIONAL. EXTERIOR PRESSURE MEASURED AT FIFTEEN PERCENT BELOW NOMINAL DESIGN STRENGTH OF SYSTEM. NO MALFUNCTION ESTABLISHED.

Run through history of stabilizer performance.

Minute by minute record, off the tapes. Identify when nose-down began and check all circuits, components, and total system status at that moment.

WORKING.

Ludongo calls, "O'Banion, why don't you use the engine's thrust to take us up just a little? There's no sense staying at this depth. . . ."

"Not necessary at this time. May be possible to identify malfunction and correct it before critical depth is reached."

Bromley asks, "Is that O'Banion talking or the computer?"

"I . . . I can't tell," Ludongo says, sounding shocked.

Speer gets up from his couch and heads for Bromley's compartment. No, not Bromley's; Ling's.

"Could I speak with you, Dr. Ling? In private?"

Ling's been running tapes of our encounter with the sharks, when they slaughtered the whale family. He blinks once at Speer, then reaches out and turns off his intercom connection. Blank now.

Where's that stabilizer history?

WORKING. SCANNING TAPES FOR COMPLETE DATA. AS INSTRUCTED.

"O'Banion, this is Ludongo again. I don't want to sound panicky, but it's getting damned uncomfortable in here. Can't you take us up at least a little way?"

Bromley, "I thought it was only me. It *is* becoming bad in here. My head aches terribly, and

I'm beginning to get pains in my chest and abdomen.''

Check internal pressure. Rising. Nearing max allowable. Check life-support systems. All functioning normal, but curves starting to approach red lines.

"Internal environment and life-support system performance are both within tolerable limits. Emotional factors may be adding to your discomfort. No one is in immediate physical danger. Suggest you ask Dr. Speer for tranquilizers.''

"He's talking like the ruddy computer!" Bromley insists.

The intercom in Speer's compartment flicks back on. Speer leaves, returns to the sick bay.

"This pressure is hurting the captain," he says, squinting at the monitor board above Voronov's head. "His breathing rate is going down steadily.''

"Check for gill malfunction." Why does someone have to spell out everything for him?

"For God's sake!" Bromley shouts. "Take us up! Can't you see that we're starting to die in here? It's too deep, we can't stand it in here for much longer!''

"All systems are within tolerable limits.''

"But the *people* aren't!" Bromley screams. "Damn the machines! The people are dying! Damn you military heroes; you're driving us to death. It was a mistake to trust our lives to you.''

"Life-support systems indicate your reaction is

purely emotional, possibly close to hysteria. Dr. Speer, please—"

"May I interrupt?" Ling's voice slides in smoothly. "Although all systems appear to be operating within tolerable limits, as you say, I suggest that there is one system that may be working at less than nominal values."

"Which one?"

"The pilot."

He means the human pilot. Operating at less than nominal value. No way to check that.

Ling goes on, "You have been at the controls steadily now for more than twelve hours. If nothing else, fatigue may be clouding your judgment. Perhaps you should check the computer for operating procedures specified for situations such as this. I believe that they call for computer control of the ship while the pilot rests."

"Computer control unfeasible during emergency situation." He should know that!

"Then perhaps you could use the engine thrust to lift us to a safer pressure level and afterward take your rest."

"Suggestion unfeasible."

Speer, "He's withdrawing more and more."

"He's becoming part of the computer," Bromley says. He's talking nonsense, but his voice sounds strangely hushed, no longer raving.

"What can we do about it?" asks Ludongo.

Nothing. They can't control the ship. They can't

get to the flight deck because the hatch is being closed and dogged down. There. They need the ship. But the ship doesn't need them. Turn off the intercom and stop their faces and voices from interfering with the ship's performance.

SYSTEMS CHECK.

Displays parading now; graphs and charts, pretty yellow curves on black backgrounds; multicolored bars creeping across white grid lines; all of them edging toward red lines, danger zones. Life-support systems, electrical power demand, navigation, control, propulsion reserve, sensors. All getting weaker, sinking deeper.

Medical monitor shows Voronov completely stable. Heart rate, breathing rate, metabolic rate, alpha rhythm: all zero.

OPERATIONAL HISTORY OF STABILIZER COMPLETED.

Display it.

NO MALFUNCTIONS IDENTIFIED. NO SYSTEM OR COMPONENT FAILURES IDENTIFIED. STABILIZER SYSTEM OPERATING WITHIN NOMINAL VALUES. ORIGIN OF PERSISTENT NOSE-DOWN ATTITUDE UNIDENTIFIED.

Insert stabilizer history in ship's log under prime priority. Important to make them realize what happened, for the mission analysis.

ONE HOUR FORTY MINUTES TO PREDICTED HULL FAILURE.

Generate a plot showing how much height would be gained by using engine thrust to counteract stabilizer failure.

WORKING. COMPLETED.

Useless. Curve doesn't even reach ocean surface. Burn out engines without getting above surface and the stabilizer will nose ship back down. Check recorder, is it ready for separation?

RECORDER SYSTEM FUNCTIONING AT NOMINAL VALUE. SEPARATION CHARGES READY FOR ARMING. WILL ARM AUTOMATICALLY ON RED ALERT, WILL FIRE AUTOMATICALLY ON MAJOR SYSTEM FAILURE.

And the rest of the recorder system?

RECORDER PROPULSION SUBSYSTEM IN STANDBY MODE. GUIDANCE SUBSYSTEM FUNCTIONAL. BEACON SUBSYSTEM FUNCTIONAL.

All major mission objectives are met if the recorder gets back to the orbiting ships.

AFFIRMATIVE. ALL MAJOR MISSION OBJECTIVES MET ALSO IF RECORDER SYSTEM SUCCESSFULLY TRANSMITS STORED DATA AND SHIP'S LOG TO RECEIVERS ABOARD ORBITAL SHIPS.

Good. Mission objectives will be met despite stabilizer malfunction and hull failure.

NO STABILIZER MALFUNCTION IDENTIFIED.

Correct.

CREW CHECK.

Crew incapacitated. Cannot be contacted.

PILOT REST PERIOD DUE IN FIVE MINUTES.

No rest period. Captain incapacitated. No other pilot available.

EMERGENCY PROCEDURE CALLS FOR PILOT TO RECEIVE NUTRIENTS AND DISCONNECT FROM ACTIVE SHIP CONTROL WHILE MAINTAINING NEURAL CONNECTION WITH COMPUTER AND SENSORS.

Guess it won't hurt anything. Tired. . . . How much time to hull failure?

ONE HOUR THIRTY-FIVE MINUTES.

Disconnecting from active ship control. Will reconnect in one hour. If no reconnection is initiated in one hour, sound yellow alert.

UNDERSTOOD.

Get nutrient tube. Last meal. Check sensors . . . completely empty out there, nothing around us. Maybe we're too deep for the whales now. . . . Sleepy. What difference will a dream make now?

Have I been asleep?

ALPHA RHYTHMS INDICATED SLEEP PATTERN.

How long?

FIFTY MINUTES ELAPSED SINCE CONTROL DISCONNECTION.

Reconnection with controls now. How much time to hull failure?

FIFTY-FIVE MINUTES.

Wait, that's wrong.

PREDICTED HULL FAILURE WILL OCCUR IN FIFTY-FIVE MINUTES.

But before I went to sleep it was one hour thirty-five. Been asleep fifty minutes, so we should have only forty-five minutes to failure, not fifty-five.

DESCENT RATE SLOWED DURING PILOT REST PERIOD.

Show me! Damn, it did level off a bit. But now it's getting as steep as ever. Why in hell . . .

SUBCONSCIOUS ACTIVITIES REPORT IS REQUIRED.

Not now, I'm thinking.

HULL FAILURE PREDICTED IN FIFTY-FOUR MINUTES WILL INITIATE RECORDER SEPARATION. FINAL SUBCONSCIOUS ACTIVITIES REPORT IS REQUIRED FOR COMPLETION OF MISSION OBJECTIVE FOURTEEN.

Damn mission objective fourteen! Oh . . . okay, I'll think while I talk.

I . . . it was the same dream. I saw Marlene die again. Only this time I recognized where it happened.

I was in my tank, watching her booster launch on the videoscreen in my compartment. I had asked to go out to the launch, but they wouldn't risk letting any of us out of the water, even in special pressure suits. Marlene was lifting off for rendezvous with the starship. He was already aboard, waiting in orbit for her, waiting to go with her to Sirius. Her booster must have malfunctioned. It exploded on the pad, I guess.

And then . . . somehow I was standing there at the pad, naked. I could feel the heat from the flames on my skin. The smoke from the explosion was swirling all around. You could hear alarm sirens and people shouting. Somebody . . . it was Bromley! He was dressed in the admiral's uniform and shouting at me, above all the noise:

"It's your fault! You killed her!"

It's cold. . . . God, I feel cold. I tried to tell him it wasn't true, I had nothing to do with it, but it all changed, shifted. I was back in that stupid office with that fat civilian telling me I had been turned down for the star missions. . . .

"I'm sorry, there are just so many berths on the starships, and we had to take the absolute cream of the crop. But there will be other missions . . ."

"I'll be too old for the next round of star flights. Too old, too old."

"No, you're still young."

"But Speer's younger than I am!" I blurted. Which was crazy, because I hadn't even met Speer yet.

INTERCOM ALARM FLASHING.

I don't want to talk to them. They're afraid to die. Everybody dies, but they don't want to face it. Voronov died and Marlene died and I'm going to die soon. Maybe it *is* my fault.

ESTIMATED TIME TO HULL FAILURE FORTY-FIVE MINUTES.

Still sinking. But dammit, she leveled off while I was asleep and disconnected. Now she's nose-down again. Give me the record of the stabilizer control settings for the past hour and a half. Manual settings and automatic.

WORKING. INTERCOM ALARM STILL FLASHING.

Okay, I'll answer it. Speer's face. He must be right on top of the camera. Sick bay couch behind him. Empty now.

"What is it?" I ask him.

He looks surprised that I answered him. "Uh . . . we've been trying to get through to you."

"You're talking to me now. What is it?"

"The captain . . ."

"I know about the captain."

"We're all in bad shape. Ling's unconscious. It's very hard to breathe . . . hard even to move around. A lot of pain . . . bad shape."

STABILIZER CONTROL SETTING RECORD AVAILABLE.

"Hold it, I'll get back to you," I tell Speer.

Look at the automatic control settings. There's the one-degree nose-down pattern, with the automatics trying to correct. But the only time they did any good . . . was while I was asleep.

What'd Ling say: *There is one system that may be working at less than nominal values.*

The pilot. Me.

Check the manual stabilizer settings. Holy Christ, it *has* been me! Manual controls depressed one degree all this time. It's been me! I've been trying to kill us!

Damned stupid computer! Why didn't you tell me I had the manual controls set nose-down?

DATA ON MANUAL SETTING WAS DISPLAYED WHEN REQUESTED, PREVIOUS INSTRUCTIONS DEALT ONLY WITH MALFUNCTION SEARCHES.

"Speer, get up here fast!" I shout.

Disconnecting from the ship controls. Let the automatics take over. I've been the weak link in the system. No wonder the computer couldn't find a malfunction. The system was working perfectly; the pilot was malfunctioning.

"I can't get the hatch open," Speer says.

Undog it. Okay, here he is, floating in and hovering alongside Voronov's couch, his face lined, eyes sunken.

STABILIZER HAS RETURNED TO LEVEL ATTITUDE. ESTIMATED TIME TO HULL FAILURE HOLDING STEADY AT THIRTY-NINE MINUTES.

"Get into the captain's couch," I tell Speer. "Stay with me. Don't leave me alone. I think we can get out of this, but I can't risk being alone up here."

He looks scared, but he does it.

Set stabilizer and all controls to return trajectory. Follow minimum energy course.

UNDERSTOOD.

Okay, execute, and show me all systems perform ance.

EXECUTING.

It looks okay. Power, propulsion, hull pressure . . . we're rising!

"We're pulling out of it," I tell Speer. "We're going to be all right."

Ludongo heard it over the intercom. "Thank all the gods of Earth!"

I see my own mouth grinning. "Bromley's got nothing to say?"

"We had to put him under sedation," Speer answers.

I try to explain to Speer what happened. He listens without a word, without even nodding.

"I guess I blamed myself for Marlene's death," I tell him. "I guess I unconsciously wanted to join her, or punish myself, or something like that."

"But how could you blame yourself for an accident? If the booster exploded, how could it be your fault?"

Ludongo breaks in, "What booster exploded? There have been no accidents among the star missions. All the ships took off on schedule. I have a friend on the Sirius mission; they didn't lose anyone in an accident."

"No, you're wrong. . . . I saw it. . . . In my

dreams I keep seeing it again. . . . The noise and flames and smoke.''

"There were no accidents.''

Could it have been just a normal lift-off I was watching? The booster rising up and out of the smoke, the flame coming from the normal rocket exhaust?

"The announcer . . . I remember now. They even showed telescopic pictures of the booster making rendezvous with the starship, in orbit. . . . It didn't explode!''

"Then why did you think she was dead?'' Speer asks.

The answer comes immediately. "She *is* dead. For me she's dead. By the time she comes back from Sirius, I'll be an old man. She'll still be about thirty-five. I've lost her for good.''

Speer, "And your dreams kept forcing you to look at the situation. They were trying to make you . . . well, wake up.''

"But I didn't want to dream.''

"Of course. You wanted to hide inside the ship, in the computer. You wanted to stop being human, because that's painful. But your dreams wouldn't let you do it.''

"But in the meantime the captain . . .''

Speer shrugs. "I don't know about the captain. I put him in the cryogenic locker; I hope that when we get back to Earth he can be revived. I think he'll be all right, but you can never tell. . . .''

Voronov's not dead! But Marlene is . . . she really is. If I ever see her again, she won't even recognize me.

SENSORS DETECT OCEAN SURFACE. ESTIMATED TIME TO SURFACE ONE HOUR THIRTY MINUTES PLUS OR MINUS FIVE PERCENT.

"Okay, back to work. Doc, you'd better check Ling and Bromley, see if they're okay. Then come back here. Dr. Ludongo, it might be a good idea to strap down. There'll be turbulence when we get closer to the surface and even more in the atmosphere."

Ludongo nods into the intercom camera. Speer pulls himself out of the captain's couch and goes aft.

We're going to make it. We're going to live. I'm going to get back to that beautiful blue planet and get rid of these damned gills and breathe sweet air again.

Give me a complete systems check.

WORKING.

Turbulence coming up. But we'll get through it. She's a good ship. I can reconnect with the controls now, it'll be okay. We'll get through the clouds and back home again.

It'll be good to be able to look at the stars again.

The Jupiter mission opened new fields of biology and planetology to the fear-driven men of Earth. But it shed no light on the Titan machines. A generation of men went to Saturn's dark satellite: scientists, soldiers, philosophers, engineers, theologians, even politicians. They tried to deduce or estimate or reason out or calculate or have revealed to them the true purpose behind the inhumanly efficient machines. From neutron beam probes to prayers, nothing worked. The machines kept their secret. And men began to realize that the answer, if it was ever found, would come from beyond the solar system.

On the starships, the generation passed in cryogenic sleep. Sidney Lee spent the years in stasis, dreaming the same relentless dream of the buildings on Titan. He didn't dream of Sylvia, or of the stars, or of the future or the past. Only of the buildings, the machines that blindly obeyed a builder who had left Earth's solar system countless millennia ago.

6. THE SIRIUS MISSION

Lee opened his eyes.

"What is it?"

Carlos Pascual was smiling down at him, his round dark-skinned face relaxed and almost happy. "We are there . . . here, I mean. We are braking, preparing to go into orbit."

Lee blinked and sat up. "We made it?"

"Yes, yes," Pascual answered softly as his eyes shifted to the bank of indicators on the console behind Lee's shoulder. "The panel claims that you are alive and well. How do you feel?"

That took a moment's thought. "A little hungry."

"A common reaction." The smile returned. "You can join the others in the galley."

The expedition's medical chief helped Lee to

swing his legs over the edge of the couch, then left him and went to the next unit, where a blond woman lay still, sleeping. With an effort, Lee recalled her: Doris McNertny, primary biologist, backup biochemist. Lee pulled a deep breath into his lungs and tried to get started. The overhead light panels, on full intensity now, made him want to squint.

Standing was something of an experiment. *No shakes*, Lee thought gratefully. The room was large and circular, with no viewports. Each of the twenty hibernation couches had been painted a different color by some psychology team back on Earth. Most of them were empty now. The remaining occupied ones had their lids off and the life-system connections removed as Pascual, Tanaka, and May Connearney worked to revive the people. Despite the color scheme, the room looked and smelled clinical.

The galley, Lee focused his thoughts, feeling momentarily like a true sixty-year-old, *is in this globe, one flight up*. The ship was built in globular sections that turned in response to g-pulls. With the main fusion engines firing to brake their approach to final orbit, "up" was temporarily in the direction of the engines' thrustors. But inside the globes it didn't make much difference.

He found the stairwell that ran through the globe. Inside the winding metal ladderway the rumbling vibrations from the ship's engines were echoing strongly enough to be heard as actual sound.

"Sid! Good morning!" Aaron Hatfield had stationed himself at the entrance to the galley and was acting as a one-man welcoming committee.

There were only a half-dozen people in the galley. *Of course,* Lee realized. *The crew personnel are at their stations.* Except for Hatfield, the people were bunched at the galley's lone viewport, staring outside and speaking in hushed subdued whispers.

"Hello, Aaron." Lee didn't feel jubilant, not after a thirty-year sleep. He tried to picture how Sylvia must look and found he couldn't do it. *She must be nearly sixty by now.*

Hatfield took his arm and towed him to the dispenser counter. "Coffee, spirits, adrenalin. . . . Take your pick."

Hatfield was the expedition's primary biochemist, a chunky, loud-speaking, overgrown kid whom it was impossible to dislike, no matter how he behaved. Lee knew that Hatfield wouldn't go near the viewport because the sight of space, of emptiness, terrified him.

"Hey, there's Doris!" Hatfield shouted to no one, and scampered to the entrance as she stepped uncertainly into the galley.

Lee dialed for coffee, and with the hot cup in his hand walked slowly toward the viewport.

"Hello, Sid," Marlene said as he came up alongside her. The others at the viewport turned and muttered their greetings.

"How close are we?" Lee asked.

Charnovsky, the geologist, answered positively, "Two days before we enter final orbit."

The stars crowded out the darkness beyond their viewport; millions of them, spattered against the blackness like droplets from a paint spray. In the faint reflection of the port's plastic Lee could see six human faces looking lost and awed.

Then the ship swung, ever so slightly, in response to some command from the crew and the computers. A single star—close and blazingly powerful—slid into view, lancing painfully brilliant light through the polarizing viewport. Lee's eyes snapped shut, but not before the glare burned its afterimage against his closed eyelids.

They all ducked back instinctively.

"Welcome to Sirius," somebody said.

Picture our solar system. Now replace the sun with Sirius A, the Dog Star: a young, blue star, nearly twice as hot and big as the sun. Take away the planet Uranus, nearly two billion kilometers from the sun, and replace it with the white dwarf Sirius B, the Pup: just as hot as Sirius A, but collapsed to a hundredth of a star's ordinary size. Now sweep away all the planets between the Dog and the Pup except two: a bald chunk of rock the size of Mercury orbiting some 100 million kilometers from A, and an Earth-sized planet some seven times farther out.

Give the Earth-sized planet a cloud-sprinkled atmosphere, a few large seas, some worn-down mountain chains, and a thin veneer of simple green life clinging to its dusty surface. Finally, throw in one lone gas giant planet, far beyond the Pup, nearly four billion kilometers from A. Add some meteroids and comets and you have the Sirius system.

"They should have named this ship *Afterthought*," Lee said to Charnovsky.

"You don't like *Sagan?*" the Russian muttered as he pushed a pawn across the board between them. They were sitting in the light-paneled rec room. A few others were scattered around the semicircular room, reading, talking, dictating messages that wouldn't reach Earth for more than eight years. Soft music purred in the background.

The Earth-like planet—officially, Sirius A-2—swung past the nearest viewport. The ship had been in orbit for nearly three weeks, and rotating about its long axis to keep a half-g feeling of weight for the scientists.

"We were sent here as an afterthought," Lee continued. "Nobody expects us to find anything. Most of the experts back on Earth didn't really believe there could be an Earth-like planet around a blue star."

"They were correct," Charnovsky said. "Your move."

Lehman, the psychiatrist, pulled up a web chair to the kibitzer's position between Lee and Charnovsky.

"Mind if I watch?" He was small but trim and athletic-looking; kept himself tanned under the UV lamps in the ship's gym room.

Within minutes they were discussing the chances of finding anything on the planet below them.

"You sound terribly pessimistic," the psychiatrist said.

"The planet looks pessimistic," Charnovsky replied "It was scoured clean when Sirius B exploded, and life has hardly had a chance to get started again on its surface."

"But it *is* Earth-like, isn't it?"

"Hah!" Charnovsky burst. "To a simple-minded robot it may seem Earth-like. The air is breathable. The chemical composition of the rocks is grossly similar. But no man would call that desert an Earth-like world. There are no trees, no grasses, it's too hot, the air is too dry. . . ."

"And the planet's too young to have evolved an intelligent species," Lee added. "Which makes me the biggest afterthought of all."

"Well, there might be something down there for an archaeologist to puzzle over," Lehman countered. "Things will look better once we get down to the surface. I think we're all getting a touch of cabin fever in here."

"Is that your professional opinion, Doctor?" Lee asked.

Before Lehman could reply, Lou D'Orazio—the ship's geophysicist and cartographer—came bounding through the hatchway of the rec room. Taking advantage of the half-gravity, he crossed to their chess table in two jumps.

"Look at this!"

He slapped a still-warm photograph on the chess table, scattering pieces over the floor. Charnovsky swore something in Slavic, and everyone in the room turned.

It was one of the regular cartographic stereo photos, crisscrossed with grid lines. It showed the shoreline of one of the planet's mini-oceans. A line of steep bluffs followed the shore.

"It looks like an ordinary . . ."

"*Aspette uno momento*. . . . Wait a minute. . . . See, here." D'Orzaio pulled a magnifier from his coverall pocket. "Look!"

Lee peered into the magnifier. Fuzzy, wavering, gray . . .

"It looks like . . ."

Lehman said, "Whatever it is, it's standing on two legs."

"It's a man," Charnovsky said flatly.

Within minutes the whole scientific staff had piled into the rec room and crowded around the table, together with all the crew members except the two on duty in the command globe. The ship's automatic cameras took twenty more photographs of the area before their orbit carried them over the horizon from the spot.

Five of the pictures showed the shadowy figure of a bipedal creature.

The spot was in darkness by the time their orbit carried them over it again. Infrared and radar sensors showed nothing.

They squinted at the pictures, handed them from person to person, talked and argued and wondered through two entire eight-hour shifts. Crewmen left for duty and returned to the rec room again. The planet turned beneath them and once again the shoreline was bathed in Sirius' hot glow. But there was no trace of the humanoid; neither the cameras, the manned telescopes, nor the other sensors could spot anything.

One by one, men and women left the rec room, sleepy and talked out. Finally, only Lee, Charnovsky, Lehman, and Captain Rassmussen were left sitting at the chess table with the finger-smudged photos spread out before them.

"They're men," Lee murmured. "Erect bipedal men."

"It's only one creature," the captain said. "And all we know is that it looks something like a man."

Rassmussen was tall, ham-fisted, rawboned, with a ruddy face that could look either elfin or Viking but nothing in between. His voice, though, was thin and high. To the everlasting gratitude of all aboard, he had fought to get a five-year supply of beer brought along. Even now, he had a mug tightly wrapped in one big hand.

"All right, they're humanoids," Lee conceded. "That's close enough."

The captain hiked a shaggy eyebrow. "I don't like jumping at shadows, you know. These pictures . . ."

"Men or not," Charnovsky said, "we must land and investigate closely."

Lee glanced at Lehman, straddling a turned-around chair and resting his arms tiredly on its back. The psychiatrist said nothing, he merely watched.

"Oh, we'll investigate," Rassmussen agreed, "but not too fast. If they are an intelligent species of some kind, we've got to go gingerly. I'm under orders from the Council, you know."

"They haven't tried to contact us," Lee said. "That means they either don't know we're here, or they're not interested, or . . ."

"Or what?"

Lee knew how it would sound, but he said it anyway. "Or they're waiting to get their hands on us."

Rassmussen laughed. "That sounds dramatic, sure enough."

"Really?" Lee heard his voice as though it were someone else's. "Suppose the humanoids down there are the same race that built the machines on Titan?"

"Nonsense," Charnovsky blurted. "There are

no cities down there, no sign whatsoever of an advanced civilization.''

The captain took a long swallow of beer. Then, ''There's no sign of Earth's civilization on the planet either, you know. Yet *we* are here, sure enough.''

Lee's insides were fluttering now. ''If they are the ones who built on Titan . . .''

''It is still nonsense!'' Charnovsky insisted. ''To assume that the first extraterrestrial creature resembling a man is representative of the race that visited the solar system hundreds of centuries ago . . . ridiculous! The statistics alone put the idea in the realm of fantasy.''

''Wait, there's more to it,'' Lee said. ''Why should a visitor from another star go to the trouble of building machines that work for centuries without stopping?''

They looked at him, waiting for him to answer his own question: Rassmussen with his Viking's craggy face, Charnovsky trying to puzzle it out in his own mind, Lehman calm and half-amused.

''The Titan buildings are more than alien,'' Lee said. ''They're hostile. Call it an assumption, a hypothesis. But I can't picture an alien race building machinery like that except for an all-important purpose. That purpose was military.''

Rassmussen looked truly puzzled now. ''Military? But who were they fighting?''

''Us,'' Lee answered. ''A previous civilization

on Earth. A culture that arose before the Ice Ages, or maybe during them, in one of the long, warm stretches in between glaciations. A human culture that went into space, met an alien civilization, and was smashed so badly that there's hardly a trace of it left.''

Charnovsky's face was reddening with the effort of staying quiet.

''I know it's conjecture.'' Lee went on quietly, ''but if there was a war between ancient man and the builders of the Titan machines, then the two cultures must have arisen close enough to each other to make war possible. Widely separated cultures can't make war, they can only contact each other every few centuries or millennia. The aliens had to come from a nearby star . . . like Sirius.''

''No, no, no!'' Charnovsky pounded a fist on his thigh. ''It's preposterous, unscientific! There is not one shred of evidence to support this . . . this pipe dream!''

''What about the ruins on Mars?'' Lee asked.

''They were built by the same race as on Titan.''

''No.'' Lee shook his head. ''I'd have never been able to decipher a completely alien language . . .''

''The Martian script has no relation to any language on Earth.''

''I know. But the *thinking* in it is human, not alien.''

''Bah.'' Charnovsky looked hopelessly disgusted.

But Rassmussen was thoughtful. ''Still . . .''

"Still it is nonsense," Charnovsky repeated. "The planet down there holds no interstellar technology. If there ever was one, it was blasted away when Sirius B exploded. Whoever is down there, he has no cities, no electronic communications, no satellites in orbit, no cultivated fields, no animal herds . . . nothing!"

"Then maybe he's a visitor too," Lee countered.

"Whatever it is," Rassmussen said, "it won't do for us to go rushing in like berserkers. Suppose there's a civilization down there that's so advanced we simply don't recognize it as such?"

Before Charnovsky could reply, the captain went on, "We have plenty of time. We will get more data about surface conditions from the robot landers and do a good deal more studying and thinking about the entire problem. Then, if conditions warrant it, we can land."

"But we don't have time!" Lee snapped. Surprised at his own vehemence, he continued, "Five years is a grain of sand compared to the job ahead of us. We have to investigate a completely alien culture and determine what its attitude is toward us. Just learning the language might take five years all by itself."

Lehman smiled easily and said, "Sid, suppose you're totally wrong about this, and whoever's down there is simply a harmless savage. What would be the shock to his culture if we suddenly drop in on him?''

"What'll be the shock to our culture if I'm right?''

Rassmussen drained his mug and banged it down on the chess table. "This is getting us nowhere. We haven't enough evidence to decide on an intelligent course of action. Personally, I'm in no hurry to go blundering into a nest of unknowns. Not when we can learn safely from orbit. As long as the beer holds out, we go slow.''

Lee pushed his chair back and stood up. "We won't learn a damned thing from orbit. Not anything that counts. We've got to go down there and study them close up. And the sooner the better.''

He turned and walked out of the rec room. *Rassmussen's spent half his life hauling scientists out to Titan and he can't understand why we have to make the most of our time here,* he raged to himself.

Halfway down the passageway to his quarters, he heard footsteps padding behind him. He knew who it would be. Turning, he saw Lehman coming toward him.

"Sacking in?'' the psychiatrist asked.

"Aren't you sleepy?''

"Completely bushed, now that you mention it.''

"But you want to talk to me,'' Lee said.

Lehman shrugged. "No hurry. . . .''

With a shrug of his own, Lee resumed walking to his room. "Come on, I'm too worked up to sleep, anyway.''

All the cubicles were more or less the same; a bunk, a desk, a tape reader, a sanitary closet. Lee took the webbed desk chair and let Lehman plop on the sighing air mattress of the bunk.

"Do you really believe this hostile alien theory? Or are you just—"

Lee slouched down in his chair and interrupted, "Let's not fool around, Rich. You're supposed to be keeping an eye on me and I've got you worried."

"It's my job to worry about everybody."

"I take my pills every day . . . to keep the paranoia away."

"That wasn't the diagnosis of your case, as you're perfectly well aware."

"So they called it something else. What're you after, Rich? Want to test my reflexes while I'm sleepy and my guard's down?"

Lehman smiled, professionally. "Look, Sid. You had a breakdown. You got over it. That's finished."

Nodding grimly, Lee added, "Except that I think there might be aliens down there plotting against me."

"That could be nothing more than a subconscious attempt to increase the importance of the archaeology department," Lehman countered.

"Horseshit," Lee said. "I came out here expecting something like this. I was looking for it. Why do you think I fought my way into the star flight program? It wasn't easy, after the breakdown. I had to push ahead of a lot of former friends."

"And leave your wife."

Sylvia's face twisted almost out of recognition, screaming through her tears, "You're just a cold sonofabitch! You don't care about me or anybody else! You don't give a damn about anybody but yourself!"

"The marriage was dead long before the star flights came up," Lee said. "This was just a good excuse to bury it. She's getting all my accumulated dividends. She'll spend her old age in comfort while we're sleeping our way back home."

"But why?" Lehman said. "Why should you give up everything—friends, family, wife, position—to get out here?"

Lee knew the answer, hesitated about putting it into words, then realized that Lehman knew it too. "Because I had to face it. I had to do what I could to find out about those buildings on Titan."

"And that's why you want to rush down there and contact whoever it is we saw?"

"Right." Lee almost wanted to laugh. "I'm hoping they can tell me if I'm crazy or not."

It was three months before they landed.

Rassmussen was thorough, patient, and stubborn. Unmanned landers sampled and tested surface conditions. Observation satellites were strung out in a network of orbits, crisscrossing the planet at the lowest possible altitude—except for one that hung in synchronous orbit over the spot where the humanoids had first been found.

That was the only place where any animal life was seen, along the shoreline for a grand distance of perhaps five kilometers. The humanoids, nothing else. And nowhere else on the planet.

Lee argued and swore and stormed at the delay. Rassmussen stayed firm. Only when the captain was satisfied that nothing more could be learned from orbit did he agree to land his ship. And still he sent clear word back toward Earth that he might be landing in a trap.

The great ship settled slowly, almost delicately, on a hot tongue of fusion plasma and touched down on the western edge of a desert some two hundred kilometers from the humanoid site. A range of rugged-looking hills separated them. The staff and crew celebrated that night. The next morning, Lee, Charnovsky, Hatfield, Doris McNertny, Alicia Monteverdi, and Marlene moved into the ship's "Sirius globe." They were to be the expedition's "outsiders," the specialists who would eventually live in the planetary environment. They represented archaeology, geology, biochemistry, biology, ecology, and atmospheric physics, with backup specialties in chemistry, paleontology, anthropology, and meteorology.

The Sirius globe held their laboratories, workrooms, equipment, and living quarters. They were quarantined from the rest of the ship's staff and crew, the "insiders," until the captain agreed that the surface conditions on the planet would be no threat to the rest of the expedition members. *That'll take two years, minimum,* Lee knew.

Gradually, the "outsiders" began to expose themselves to the local environment. They began to breathe the air, acquire the microbes. Pascual and Tanaka made them sit in the medical examination booths twice each day, and even checked them personally every other day. The two M.D.'s wore disposable biosuits and worried expressions when they entered the Sirius globe. The medical computers compiled miles of data tapes on each of the six "outsiders," but still Pascual's normally pleasant face acquired a perpetual frown of anxiety.

"I just don't like the idea of this damned armor," Lee grumbled.

He was already encased up to his neck in a gleaming white powersuit, the type that crew members wore when working outside the ship in vacuum. Aaron Hatfield and Marlene were helping to check out all the seams and connections. A few feet away, in the cramped "locker room," Alicia Monteverdi looked as though she were being swallowed by an oversized automaton. Charnovsky and Doris were checking her suit.

"It's for your own protection," Marlene told Lee in a throaty whisper as she applied a test meter to the radio panel on his suit's chest. "You and Alicia won the toss for the first trip outside, but this is the price you must pay. Now be a good boy and don't complain.''

Lee had to grin. *"Ja, Fraulein Schulmeisterein."*

She looked at him with a rueful smile. "Thank God you never had to carry on a conversation in German.''

Finally Lee and Alicia clumped through the double hatch into the airlock. It took another fifteen minutes for them to perform the final checkout, but at last they were ready. The outer hatch slid back and they started down the long ladder to the planet's surface. The armored suits were equipped with muscle-amplifying power systems, so that even a girl as tiny as Alicia could handle their bulk easily.

Lee went down the ladder first and set foot on the ground. It was bare and dusty, the sky a reddish haze. *The grand adventure,* he thought. *All the expected big moments in life are flops.* A hot breeze hummed in his earphones. It was early morning, Sirius hadn't cleared the barren horizon yet, although the sky was fully bright. Despite the suit's air conditioning, Lee felt the heat.

He reached up a hand as Alicia climbed warily down the last few steps of the ladder. The plastic rungs gave under the suit's weight, then slowly straightened themselves when the burden was removed.

"Well," he said, looking at her wide-eyed face

through the transparent helmet of her suit, "what do you think of it?"

"It's hardly paradise, is it?"

"Looks like it's leaning the other way," Lee said.

They explored. Lee and Alicia that first day, then the other "outsiders," shuffling ponderously inside their armor. Lee chafed against the restriction of the powersuits, but Rassmuseen insisted and would brook no argument. They went timidly at first, never out of sight of the ship. Charnovsky chipped samples from rock outcroppings, while the others took air and soil samples, dug for water, searched for life.

"The perfect landing site," Doris complained after a hot, tedious day. "There's no form of life bigger than a yeast mold within a hundred kilometers of here."

It was a hot world, a dry world, a brick-dust world where the sky was always red. Sirius was a blowtorch searing down on them, too bright to look at even through the polarized visors of their suits. At night there was no moon to see, but the Pup bathed this world in a deathly bluish glow far brighter yet colder than moonlight. The night sky was never truly dark, and only a few strong stars could be seen from the ground.

Through it all, the robot satellites relayed more pictures of the humanoids along the seacoast. They appeared almost every day, usually only briefly. Sometimes there were a few of them, sometimes only one, once there were nearly a dozen. The highest resolution photos showed them to be human in size and build. But what their faces looked like, what they wore, what they were *doing*—all escaped the drone cameras.

The robot landers, spotted in a dozen scattered locations within a thousand kilometers of the ship, faithfully recorded and transmitted everything they were programmed to look for. They sent pictures and chemical analyses of plant life and insects. But no higher animals.

Alicia's dark eyes looked perpetually puzzled, Lee saw. "It makes no sense," she would say. "There's nothing on this planet more advanced than insects . . . yet there are men. It's as though humans suddenly sprang up in the Silurian period on Earth. They *can't* be here. I wish we could examine the life in the seas . . . perhaps that would tell us more."

"You mean those humanoids didn't originate on this planet," Lee said to her.

She shook her head. "I don't know. I don't see how they could have . . ."

Gradually they pushed their explorations farther afield, beyond the ship's limited horizon. In the motorized powersuits a man could cover more than a hundred kilometers a day, if he pushed it. Lee always headed toward the grizzled hills that separated them from the seacoast. He helped others to dig, to collect samples, but he always pointed them toward the sea.

"The satellite pictures show some decent greenery on the seaward side of the hills," he told Doris. "That's where we should go."

Rassmussen wouldn't move the ship. He wanted his base of operations, his link homeward, at least a hundred kilometers from the nearest possible threat. But finally he relaxed enough to allow the scientists to go out overnight and take a look at the hills.

And maybe the coast, Lee added silently to the captain's orders.

Rassmussen decided to let them use one of the ship's two air-cushion vehicles. He assigned Jerry Grote, the chief engineer, and Chien Shu Li, electronics specialist, to handle the skimmer and take command of the trip. They would live in biosuits and remain inside the skimmer at all times. Lee, Marlene, Doris, and Charnovsky made the trip. Grote did the driving and navigating; Chien handled communications and the computer.

It took a full day's drive to get to the hills. Grote, a lanky, lantern-jawed New Zealander, decided to camp at the base of the hills as night came on.

"I thought you'd be a born mountaineer," Lee poked at him.

Grote leaned back in his padded driver's seat and planted a large slippered foot on the skimmer's control panel.

"I could climb those wrinkles out there in my sleep," he said pleasantly. "But we've got to be careful of this shiny vehicle, don't we?"

From the driver's compartment, Lee could see Marlene pushing forward toward them, squeezing between the racks of electronics gear that separated the forward compartment from the living and working quarters.

Even in the drab coveralls, she showed a nice profile.

"I'd like to go outside," she said to Grote. "We've been sitting all day like tourists in a shuttle."

Grote nodded. "Got to wear a hard suit, though."

"But . . ."

"Orders."

She glanced at Lee, then shrugged. "All right."

"I'll come with you," Lee said.

Squirming into the armored suits in the aft hatchway was exasperating, but at last they were ready and Lee opened the hatch. They stepped across the tail fender of the skimmer and jumped to the dusty ground.

"Being inside this is almost worse than being in the car," Marlene said.

They walked around the skimmer. Lee watched his shadow lengthen as he placed the setting Sirius at his back.

"Look . . . *look!*"

He saw Marlene pointing and turned to follow

her gaze. The hills rising before them were dazzling with a million sparkling lights: red and blue and white and dazzling, shimmering lights as though a cascade of precious jewels were pouring down the hillsides.

"What is it?" Marlene's voice sounded excited, thrilled, not the least afraid.

Lee stared at the shifting multicolored lights. It was like playing a lamp on cut crystal. He took a step toward the hills, then looked down to the ground. From inside the cumbersome suit it was hard to see the ground close to your feet and harder still to bend down and pick up anything. But he squatted slowly and reached for a small stone. Getting up again, Lee held the stone high enough for it to catch the fading rays of daylight.

The rock glittered with a shower of varicolored sparkles.

"They're made of glass," Lee said.

Within minutes Charnovsky and Doris were out of the car to marvel at it. The Russian collected as many rocks as he could stuff into his suit's thigh pouches. Lee helped him; the women merely stood by the skimmer and watched the hills blaze with lights.

Sirius disappeared below the horizon at last, and the show ended. The hills returned to being brownish, erosion-worn slumps of rock.

"Crystal mountains," Marlene marveled as they returned to the skimmer.

"Not crystal," Charnovsky corrected. "Glazed rock. Granitic, no doubt. Probably melted when the Pup exploded. Atmosphere might have blown away, and the rock cooled very rapidly."

Lee could see Marlene's chin rise stubbornly inside the transparent dome of her suit. "I name them the Crystal Mountains," she said firmly.

Grote had smuggled a bottle along with them, part of his personal stock. "My most precious possession," he rightfully called it. But for the Crystal Mountains he dug it out of its hiding place and they toasted the discovery and the name. Marlene smiled and insisted that Lee also be toasted, as co-discoverer.

Hours later, Lee grew tired of staring at the metal ceiling of the sleeping quarters a few centimeters above his top-tier bunk. Even Grote's drinks didn't help him to sleep. He kept wondering about the humanoids, what they were doing, where they were from, how he would get to learn their secrets. As quietly as he could, he slipped down from his bunk. The two men beneath him were breathing evenly and deeply. Lee headed for the rear hatch, past the women's bunks.

The hard suits were standing at stiff attention, flanking both sides of the rear hatch. Lee was in his coveralls. He strapped on a pair of boots, slid the hatch open as quietly as he could and stepped out onto the fender.

The air was cool and clean, the sky bright enough

for him to make out the worn old hills. There were a few stars in the sky, but the hills didn't reflect them.

He heard a movement behind him. Turning, he saw Marlene.

"Did I wake you?"

"I'm a very light sleeper. Remember?"

"Sorry, I didn't. . . ."

"No, I'm glad you did." She shook her head slightly, and Lee noticed once again the sweep and softness of her hair. The light was too dim to make out its color, but he knew it was auburn, knew the feel of it, the scent of it.

"Besides," she was whispering, "I've been waiting for a chance to get outside without being in one of those damned suits."

He helped her down from the fender and they walked a little way from the skimmer.

"It's been a long time since we've been alone together," Lee said.

"More than three years. Since Titan . . . all that time in the Training Center."

"I know. I've been pretty lousy to you, haven't I?"

She grinned. "Yes."

"I'm sorry. There was just too much pressing on me . . . with Sylvia and the training and the exams . . . I just couldn't . . . ." He felt tongue-tied.

"I know, Sid. I didn't like it while it was happening, but it's all in the past now." She walked a little bit away from him.

"All in the past? What does that mean?"

Shrugging, she answered, "Simply that we're here and the time is now. What's done is done."

Lee looked at her, trying to determine what she meant from the expression on her face.

"Can we see the sun?" she asked, looking skyward.

"I'm not sure. I think maybe . . . there . . ." He pointed to a second-magnitude star shining alone in the grayish sky.

"Where, which one?"

He took her by the shoulder with one hand so that she could see where he was pointing.

"Oh yes, I see it."

She turned and she was in his arms and he kissed her.

"Oh, Sid . . . I've waited so long."

"I've wanted you too, Marlene . . . but there's so much . . . so much . . ."

"Shh . . . don't talk, don't say anything . . . not a word. . . ."

If any of the others suspected that Lee and Marlene had spent the night outside, they didn't mention it. All six of them took their regular pre-breakfast checks in the medical booth, and by the time they were finished eating in the cramped galley the computer had registered a safe green light for each of them.

Lee slid from the galley's folding table and made his way forward. Grote was slouched in the driver's seat, his lanky frame a geometry of knees and elbows. He was studying the viewscreen map.

"Looking for a pass through these hills for our vehicle," he said absently, his eyes on the slowly moving photo-map.

"Why take the skimmer?" Lee asked, sitting on the chair beside him. "We can cross these hills in the powersuits."

Grote cocked an eye at him. "You're really set on getting to the coast, aren't you?"

"Aren't you?"

That brought a grin.

"Of course," Lee said, almost seriously, "your orders are to stay inside the skimmer. Or do you think being inside a powersuit wouldn't bend those orders too much?"

Laughing, Grote asked, "How much do you think we ought to carry with us?"

They split the team into three groups. Chien and Charnovsky stayed with the car. Marlene and Doris would go with Lee and Grote to study the flora and fauna (if any) on the shore side of the hills. Lee and the engineer carried a pair of video camera packs with them, to set up close to the shoreline.

"Beware of the natives," Charnovsky's voice grated in Lee's earphones as they walked away from the skimmer. "They might swoop down on you with bows and arrows!" His laughter showed what he thought of Lee's theories.

Climbing the hills wasn't as bad as Lee had thought it would be. The powersuits did most of the work, and the glassy rock wasn't slippery enough to cause real troubles with footing. It was hot, though, even with the suit's cooling blowers turned up to full blast. Sirius blazed overhead, and the rocks beat glare and heat back into their faces as they climbed.

It took most of the day to get over the crest of the hills. But finally, with Sirius edging toward the horizon behind them, Lee saw the water.

The sea spread to the farther horizon, cool and blue, with long gentle swells that steepened into surf as they ran up toward the land. And the land was green here: shrubs and mossy-looking plants were sprinkled around patchily.

"Look! Look here!" Doris' voice.

Lee turned his head and saw her clumsily sinking to her knees, like an armor-plated elephant getting down ponderously to do a circus trick. She knelt beside a fernlike plant. They all walked over and helped her to photograph it, snip a leaf from it, probe its root system.

"It's the most advanced form of life we've found yet," Doris said proudly.

Aside from the men, Lee thought.

"Might as well sleep here tonight," Grote said. "I'll take the first watch."

"Can't we set the scanners to give an alarm if anything approaches?" Marlene asked. "There's nothing here that's dangerous enough to . . ."

"I want one of us awake at all times," Grote said firmly. "And nobody outside of their suits."

"There's no place like home," Doris muttered. "But after a while even your own smell gets to you."

The women lay down, locking the suits into roughly reclining positions. To Lee they looked like oversized beetles that had gotten stuck on their backs. It didn't look possible for them to get up again. Then he looked at Marlene and another thought struck him. He chuckled to himself. *Super chastity belts*.

He sat down, cranked the suit's torso section back to a comfortable reclining angle, and tried to doze off. He was dreaming of the buildings on Titan again when Grote's voice in his earphones woke him up.

"Is it my turn?" he mumbled groggy.

"Not yet. But turn off your transmitter. You were groaning in your sleep. Don't want to wake up the girls, do you?"

Lee took the second watch and simply stayed awake until daybreak without bothering any of the others. They began marching toward the sea.

The hills descended only slightly into a rolling plateau that went on until they reached the bluffs that overlooked the sea. A few hundred feet down was a narrow strip of beach, with breakers surging in.

"This is as far as we go," Grote said.

The women spent the morning collecting plant

samples. Doris found a few insects and grew more excited over them than she had about the shrubbery. Lee and Grote walked alongside the edge of the cliffs, looking for a good place to set up their cameras.

"You're sure this is the area where they were seen?" Lee asked.

The engineer turned his head inside the plastic helmet. Lee could see he was on edge, too.

"I know how to read a map, Sid."

"Sorry, I'm just anxious. . . ."

"So am I."

They walked until Sirius was almost directly overhead, a pitiless white furnace trying to melt them. They saw nothing except the constant sea, the beach, and the spongy-looking plants that huddled close to the ground.

"Not even a damned tree for shade," Grote grumbled.

They turned back and headed for the spot where they had left the women. Far up the beach, Lee saw a tiny dark spot.

"What's that?"

Grote stared for a few moments. "Probably a rock."

"Wasn't there before." Lee touched a button on the chest of his suit and an electro-optical viewpiece slid down in front of his eyes. Grote did the same. Turning a dial on the suit's control panel, Lee tried to focus on the spot. It wavered in the heat currents of the early afternoon, blurred and uncertain. Then it seemed to jump out of view.

Lee punched the button and the lens slid away from his eyes. "It's moving!" he shouted, and started to run.

He heard Grote's heavy breathing as the engineer followed him and the electrical hum of the suit's tiny motors as they both nearly flew in the powersuits along the edge of the cliffs, covering a dozen meters with each stride.

It was a man! No, not one, Lee saw, but two of them walking along the beach, their feet in the foaming water.

"Get down, you bloody fool!" he heard Grote shrilling at him.

He dove headlong, bounced, cracked the back of his head against the helmet's plastic, then banged his chin on the soft inner lining of the collar.

"Don't want them to see us, do you?" Grote was whispering now.

"They can't hear us, for God's sake," Lee said into his suit radio.

They wormed their way to the cliff's edge again and watched. The two men seemed to be dressed in black. But with the electro-optical viewers, Lee saw that they were black-skinned and naked.

After a hurried council, they unslung one of the video cameras and its power unit, set it up right there, turned it on, and then backed away from the edge of the cliff. Then they ran as hard as they could, staying out of sight of the beach, with the remaining camera. They passed the startled women and breathlessly shouted out their find. The women dropped their work and started running after them.

About a kilometer or so farther on they dropped to all fours again and cautiously crawled to the edge once more. Grote hissed the women into silence as they hunched up beside him.

The beach was empty now.

"Do you think they saw us?" Lee asked.

"Don't know."

Lee used the electro-optics again and scanned the beach. "No sign of them."

"Footprints!" Grote snapped. "Look there!"

The trails of two very human-looking sets of footprints marched straight into the water. All four of them searched the sea for more than an hour, but saw nothing. Finally they decided to set up the other camera. It was turning dark by the time they finished.

"We've got to get back to the car," Grote said wearily when they finished. "There's not enough food in the suits for another day."

"I'll stay here," Lee replied. "You can bring me more supplies tomorrow."

"No. If there's anything to see, the cameras will pick it up. Chien's monitoring them back at the car, and the whole crew of the ship must be watching the view."

Lee saw there was no use arguing. Besides, he

was bone-tired. But he knew he'd be back again as soon as he could get here.

"Well, it settles a three-hundred-year-old argument," Aaron Hatfield said as they watched the viewscreen.

The biochemist and Lee were sitting in the main workroom of the ship's Sirius globe, watching the humanoids as televised by the cameras on the cliffs. Charnovsky was on the other side of the room, at a workbench, flashing rock samples with a laser so that a spectrometer could analyze their chemical composition. The other "outsiders" were traveling in the skimmer again, collecting more floral and insect specimens.

"What argument?" Lee asked.

Hatfield shifted in his chair, making the webbing creak. "About the human form . . . whether it's an accident or the result of evolutionary selection. From *them*," he nodded toward the screen, "I'd say it's no accident."

One camera was on wide-field focus, and showed a group of three men. They were wading hip-deep in the mild surf, carrying slender rods high above their heads to keep them free of the surging waves. The other camera was fixed on a close-up view of three women standing on the beach, watching their men.

They looked almost completely human. Their faces were slightly different: broader, heavier, with noticeable brow ridges. Their skins were black.

They were almost completely hairless. And entirely naked.

Every morning they appeared on the beach, often carrying the rods, but sometimes not. Lee concluded that they must live in caves cut into the cliffs. The rods looked like simple bone spears, but even under the closest focus of the cameras he couldn't be sure.

"If I didn't know better," Lee muttered, more to himself than anyone else, "I'd almost say they were Neanderthals."

"Neanderthals?" Hatfield echoed. "But Neanderthals were shaggy and shambling . . . more like an ape, weren't they?"

Lee shook his head. "Of course not. Nobody knows what their hair and skin coloring was. And they might have been squatter and shorter than these people, but then again . . . hell, I wish we had an anthropologist here."

"I thought you were the anthropology expert."

"What I know about anthropology you could stuff in Rassmussen's beer mug and still have room for two pints. Who knew we'd run into *people?* Everybody was expecting six-legged purple things."

Charnovsky came over and pulled up a chair. "So. Have they caught any fish yet this morning?"

"Not yet," Lee answered.

Jabbing a stubby finger toward the screen, the Russian asked, "Are these the geniuses who built the machines on Titan? Fishing with bone spears? They don't make much of an enemy, Lee."

"They could have been our enemy," Lee answered, forcing a thin smile. He was getting accustomed to Charnovsky's needling, but not reconciled to it.

The geologist shook his head sadly. "Take the advice of an older man, dear friend, and disabuse yourself of this idea. Statistics are a powerful tool, Lee. The chances of this particular race being the one that built on Titan are fantastically high. And the chances . . ."

"What're the chances of two intelligent races both evolving along the same physical lines?" Lee snapped.

Charnovsky shrugged. "We have two known races. They are both human in form. The chances must be excellent."

Lee turned back to watch the viewscreen, then asked Hatfield, "Aaron, the biochemistry is the same as Earth's, isn't it?"

"Very close."

"I mean . . . I could eat local food and be nourished by it? I wouldn't be poisoned or anything like that?"

"Well-l-l," Hatfield said, visibly thinking it out as he spoke, "as far as the structure of the proteins and other foodstuffs are concerned . . . yes, I guess you could get away with eating it. The biochemistry is basically the same as ours, as nearly as I've been able to tell. But so are terrestrial shellfish, and they make me deathly ill. You see, there're all sorts of enzymes, and microbial parasites, and viruses. . . ."

"We've been living with the local bugs for months now," Lee said. "We're adapted to them, aren't we?"

"You know what they say about visiting strange places: don't drink the water."

One of the natives struck into the water with his spear and instantly the water began to boil with the thrashing of some sea creature. The other two men drove their spears home and the thrashing died. They lifted a four-foot long fish out of the water and started back for the beach, carrying it triumphantly over their heads. The camera's autotracker kept the picture on them. The women on the beach were jumping and clapping with joy.

"Damn," Lee said softly. "They're as human as we are."

"And obviously representative of a high technical civilization," Charnovsky said.

"Survivors of such a culture, maybe," Lee answered. "Their culture might have been wiped out by the Pup's explosion. . . . Or by war."

"Ah, now it gets even more dramatic: two cultures destroyed, ours *and* theirs."

"All right, go ahead and laugh," Lee said. "I won't be able to prove anything until I get to live with them."

"Until what?" Hatfield said.

"Until I go out there and meet them face to face, learn their language, their culture, live with them."

Late that night, after hours of pacing the tiny cubicle that was his quarters, Lee phoned Marlene.

"I have to talk to you," he said.

Her face on the small phonescreen seemed puzzled, almost worried. "It's pretty late, Sid, and honestly, I'm nearly wiped out. Doris and I have been outside all day . . ."

"It's important," he said. "It won't take long."

She smiled at that and suddenly *he* felt puzzled.

"All right," Marlene said. "If it won't take long."

He padded barefoot down the dim, night-lit passageway to her door. She opened it when he tapped at it.

She was grinning. "I haven't done anything like this since I left the dorm at CalTech."

The remark didn't register with Lee. He sat down on the only chair in the compartment and began telling her about his plans. Slowly her smile faded and she sat on the bunk and listened.

"It's the only thing we can do," he finished. "I've got to go down there and live with them, find out about them. I've *got* to."

For the first time, he looked straight at her.

"What do you want me to say?" she asked.

"I . . ." Then he shrugged.

She said, "Your mind's made up. You want to go and live with them. Why come in the middle of the night to tell me? What do you expect me to do about it?"

"I . . . well, I wanted you to know. It's something I've got to do, Marlene."

She was controlling herself carefully. Lee knew that her calm expression and soft voice were a mask. Her hands were twining together, fingers locking together and unlocking.

"All right," she said. "If you want me to admit that I'd rather not see you do it, I'll admit it. Why did you come and tell me, Sid? Was it to find an excuse for not going, or to have your ego boosted by having me beg you not to go, or just to see how much you can hurt me?"

"Hurt you?" He felt stunned.

"Oh . . ." Now there was turmoil in her eyes. "You know I don't want you to go. It *is* dangerous, and I don't want to lose you, not again, not for a second. It's hard enough to be with you every day and night with all these other people crowded around us. . . . No, I don't want you to go. But I know you will. So that's where it is. Now why don't you just get out of here and let me cry in private."

"Marlene, I didn't want to hurt you. . . . I just thought you ought to know before I told anybody else. I thought I owed you that much."

"More, Sid. A hell of a lot more, you owe. But not to me. To yourself. Now go on, get out. Leave me alone."

Baffled, he got up from the web chair and went to the door. He hesitated there for an uncertain moment, looked back toward her. She was sitting on the edge of the bunk, nearly doubled over in a tight knot of misery, staring at the floor.

"Marlene . . ."

She wouldn't answer, wouldn't even look up at him.

"I'm sorry. I've got to do this. I'll be back. . . ."

Her only response was to shake her head.

"Live with them?" Rassmussen looked startled, the first time Lee had seen him jarred. The captain's monomolecular biosuit gave his craggy face a faint sheen, like the beginnings of a sweat.

They were sitting around a circular table in the conference room of the Sirius globe: the "outsiders," plus Grote, Chien, Captain Rassmussen, Pascual, and Lehman. But Marlene wasn't there; she hadn't left her room all day.

"Aren't you afraid they might put you in a pot and boil you?" Grote asked, grinning.

"I don't think they have pots. Or fire, for that matter," Lee countered.

The laugh turned on Grote.

Lee went on quietly, "I've checked it out with Aaron, here. There's no biochemical reason why I couldn't survive in the native environment. Doris and Alicia have agreed to gather the same types of food we've seen the humanoids carrying, and I'll go on a strictly native diet for a few weeks before I go to live with them.''

Lehman hunched forward, from across the table. ''About the dynamics of having a representative of our relatively advanced culture step into their primitive—''

''I won't be representing an advanced culture to them,'' Lee said. ''I intend to be just as naked and toolless as they are. And just as black. Aaron can inject me with the proper enzymes to turn my skin black.''

''That would be necessary in any event if you don't want to die of sunstroke,'' Pascual said.

Hatfield added, ''You'll need contact lenses that'll screen out the excess UV and protect your eyes.''

''But you don't look like the natives,'' Alicia said. ''You're taller and slimmer and . . . well, handsomer!''

They all laughed again.

''I've already talked to Tanaka about that,'' Lee said. ''He can ugly me up a little . . . add some weight to my brows and cheekbones. Just temporary, not really plastic surgery in the permanent sense.''

They spent an hour discussing all the physical precautions he would have to take. Lee kept glancing up to see if Marlene would put in an appearance. Then he noticed Rassmussen frowning. *The idea's slipping out from under his control. He can't stop it now.* The captain watched each speaker in turn, squinting with concern and sinking deeper into his Viking scowl. Then, when Lee was certain that the captain could no longer object, Rassmussen spoke up:

"One more question: Are you willing to give up an eye for this mission of yours?"

"What do you mean?"

The captain's hands seemed to wander loosely without a mug of beer to tie them down. "Well . . . you seem to be willing to run a good deal of personal risk to live with these, eh, people. From the expedition's viewpoint, you will also be risking our only archaelogist and anthropologist, you know. I think the wise thing to do, in that case, would be to make sure we have a running record of everything you see and hear."

Lee nodded slowly.

"So we can swap one of your eyes for a video camera, and plant a transmitter somewhere in your skull. I'm sure there's enough empty space in your head to accommodate them." The captain chuckled toothily at his joke. Everyone else stayed silent.

Then Pascual said, "We can't do an eye procedure here. It's much too risky."

"Oh, I thought Dr. Tanaka was quite expert in surgery," the captain said. "And naturally we'd preserve the eye and restore it afterwards. Unless, of course, Professor Lee . . ." He let the suggestion dangle.

Lee looked at them sitting around the big table: Rassmussen, trying to look noncommittal; Pascual, upset and nearly angry; and Lehman, staring intently right back into Lee's eyes.

You're trying to force me to back down, Lee thought of Rassmussen. Then, of Lehman, *And if I don't back down, you'll be convinced I'm insane.*

For a long moment there was no sound in the crowded conference room except the faint whir of the air blower.

"All right," Lee said. "If Tanaka is willing to tackle the surgery, so am I."

When Lee returned to his cubicle, the message light under the phonescreen was blinking red. He flopped on the bunk, propped a pillow under his head, and asked the computer, "What's the phone message?"

The screen lit up: PLS CALL DR. LEHMAN.

My son, the psychiatrist. "Okay," he said aloud, "get him."

A moment later Lehman's tanned face filled the screen.

"I was expecting you to call," Lee said.

The psychiatrist nodded. "You agreed to pay a big price just to get loose among the natives."

"Tanaka can handle the surgery," Lee answered evenly.

"It'll be months before you're fit to leave the ship again."

"You know what our Norse captain says . . . we'll stay as long as the beer holds out."

Lehman smiled. *Professional technique*, Lee thought.

"Sid, do you really think you can mingle with these people without causing any cultural impact? Without changing them?"

Shrugging, "I don't know. I hope so. As far as we know, they're the only humanoid group on the planet. They may have never seen a stranger before."

"That's what I mean," Lehman said. "Don't you feel that . . ."

"Let's cut the circling, Rich. You know why I want to see them firsthand. If we had the time I'd study them remotely for a good long while before trying any contact. But it gets back to the beer supply. We've got to squeeze a century's worth of work into a little more than four years."

"There will be other expeditions, after we return to Earth and tell them about these people."

"Yeah. But not for thee and me, friend."

Lehman didn't answer.

"Besides," Lee went on, "by then it might be too late."

"Too late for what?"

His neck was starting to hurt; Lee hunched up to a sitting position on the bunk. "For them. Figure it out. There can't be more than fifty people in the group we've been watching. I've only seen a couple of children. And there aren't any other groups of people anywhere on the planet. They're dying out. This gang is the last of their kind. By the time another expedition gets here, there might not be any of them left.''

For once, Lehman looked surprised. "Do you really think so?"

"Yes. And before they die, we have to get some information out of them.''

"What do you mean?"

"They might not be natives of this planet," Lee said, forcing himself to speak calmly, keeping his face a mask, freezing any emotion inside of him. "They probably came from somewhere else. That somewhere is the home of the people who built the Titan machines . . . their real home. We've got to find out where it is." *Flawless logic.*

Lehman tried to smile again. "That's assuming your theory about an ancient war is right."

"Yes. Assuming I'm right."

"Assume you are," Lehman said. "And assume you find what you're looking for. Then what? Do we just take off and go back to Earth? What happens to the people here?"

"I don't know," Lee said, Titan-cold inside. "The main problem will be how to deal with the homeworld of their people.''

"But the people here, do we just let them die out?"

"I guess so. Why not? Their own people abandoned them. We don't owe them anything."

Lehman's smile was completely gone now. His face didn't look pleasant at all.

It took four months.

The surgery was difficult. And beneath all the pain was Lee's rooted fear that he would never have his sight fully restored. While he was recovering, before he was allowed out of his infirmary bed, Hatfield turned his skin black with enzyme injections. He was also fitted with a single quartz contact lens for his real eye, and a prosthetic eye that hid the submolar video camera that now hung in his emptied socket.

Through it all Marlene stayed close to him. Through the weeks of pain she was never farther away than his voice could reach. As he grew stronger, was allowed out of bed to walk around the infirmary, she stayed near.

They were eating together in his infirmary room one afternoon when he realized she was staring at him.

"Still think I look ugly?"

She looked startled for a moment. "What? Why do you say that?"

"You were staring."

"Oh . . . I was daydreaming . . . being jealous, actually."

"Jealous."

Nodding, "Feeling sorry for myself. Because you think more of those humanoids out there than you do of me."

He wanted to laugh, but didn't. "Now that's a typically feminine attitude."

"Well, you're going to live with them and leaving me behind. You've let them change your face and your skin. . . ."

With a grin he answered, "Well, Alicia doesn't seem to mind that. She says it makes me look more interesting. Savage."

"That little bitch," Marlene spat.

"Hey!"

"Oh, I've been watching her. You're not the only one she's after. Our little patrician with the blood of the conquistadors. She's an alley cat."

"Talk about feminine attitudes!"

"Well, I'm female," Marlene said, grinning herself now. "If you haven't noticed."

"Hmm . . . I guess you might be at that. Come over here," he patted the bed, "and let me study the problem a little more closely."

She got up from her chair and sat next to him on the bed. "Dr. Tanaka might not approve of this."

"You know what he can do, don't you?"

Later, as he lay back and looked at her beautiful face, he muttered, "I really don't deserve you at all."

She didn't answer. He never said it again.

* * *

Rasmussen still plodded. Long after Lee felt strong enough to get going again, he was still confined to the ship. When his complaints grew loud enough, they let him start on a diet of native foodstuffs. The medics and Hatfield hovered around him while he spent a miserable two weeks with dysentery. Then it passed. But it took a while to build up his strength again; all he had to eat now were fish, insects, and pulpy greens, raw.

After more tests, conferences, a two-week trial run out by the Crystal Mountains, and then still more exhaustive physical exams, Rasmussen at last agreed to let Lee go.

They left quickly, abruptly, before the captain could change his mind. Lee's only real farewell was to Marlene, in her room.

"You're going? When?"

"In about fifteen minutes, if Grote can check out the skimmer that fast."

She stared at him for a long moment as he stood in the doorway of the tiny cubicle. She looked as though there were a thousand things she wanted to say. But she merely put her hand to his smoke-black cheek and asked:

"Will you come back to me?"

"I'll be back," he said.

She started to say something else, her voice caught, and she turned away. Lee hesitated, then left her there with her head down and her back to him.

Grote piloted the skimmer the long way around the Crystal Mountains, down a gentle slope to the sea, through the surf and out onto the easy, billowing sea. They kept far enough out at sea for the beach to be always beyond their horizon.

When night fell, Grote nosed the skimmer landward. They came ashore around midnight, with the engines clamped down to near silence, a few kilometers up the beach from the humanoids' site. Grote, encased in a powersuit, walked with him partway and buried a relay transceiver in the sand, to pick up signals from the camera and transceiver embedded in Lee's skull.

"Good luck." Grote's voice was muffled by the helmet. Lee stood naked beside him.

He watched the New Zealander plod mechanically back into the darkness. He strained to hear the skimmer as it turned and slipped back to sea, but he could neither see nor hear it.

He was alone on the beach.

Clouds were drifting landward, riding smoothly overhead. The breeze on the beach, though, was blowing warmly out of the desert, spilling over the bluffs and across the sand, out to sea. The sparse stars of this world's sky peeped through the clouds, in and out. Along the foot of the cliffs it was deep black. Except for the wind and surf, there wasn't a sound: not a bird nor a nocturnal cat, not even an insect's chirrup.

Lee stayed near the water's edge. He wasn't

cold, even though naked. Still, he could feel himself trembling.

Grote's out there, he told himself. *If you need him, he can come roaring up the beach in ten minutes.*

But he knew he was really alone.

The clouds thickened and began to sprinkle rain, a warm, soft shower. Lee blinked the drops away from his eyes and walked slowly, a hundred paces in one direction, then a hundred paces back again.

The rain stopped as the sea horizon started turning bright. The clouds wafted away. The sky lightened first gray, then almost milky white. Lee looked toward the base of the cliffs. Dark shadows dotted the rugged cliff face. Caves. Some of them were ten meters or more above the sand.

Sirius edged a limb above the horizon and Lee, squinting, turned away from its brilliance. He looked back at the caves again, feeling the warmth of the hot star's might on his back.

The first ones out of the cave were two children, boys. They tumbled out of the same cave, off to Lee's left, giggling and running.

When they saw Lee they stopped dead. As though someone had turned them off. Lee could feel his heart beating as they stared at him. He stood just as still as they did, perhaps a hundred meters from them. They looked about five and ten years old, he judged. *If their lifespans are the same as ours*.

The taller of the two boys took one step toward

Lee, then turned and ran back into the cave. The younger boy followed him.

For several minutes nothing happened. Then Lee heard voices echoing from inside the cave. Angry? Frightened? *They're not laughing.*

Four men appeared at the mouth of the cave. Their hands were empty. They simply stood there, and gaped at him, from the shadows of the cave's mouth.

Now we'll start learning their customs about strangers, Lee thought to himself.

Very deliberately, he turned away from them and took a few steps up the beach. Then he stopped, turned again, and walked back to his original spot.

Two of the men disappeared inside the cave. The other two stood there. Lee couldn't tell what the expressions on their faces meant. They *were* faintly like the reconstructions of Neanderthals that he had seen as a student; but these were men: alive, wary, lips set in firm strength, eyes watching him.

Suddenly other people appeared at a few of the other cave mouths. *They're interconnected,* Lee realized.

He tried to smile and waved. There were women among the onlookers now, and a few children. One of the boys who saw him first—at least, it looked like him—started chattering to an adult. The man silenced him with a brusque gesture, never taking his eyes off Lee.

It was getting hot. Lee could feel perspiration trickling along his ribs as Sirius climbed above the horizon and shone straight at the cliffs. Slowly, he squatted down on the sand.

A few of the men from the first cave stepped out onto the beach. Two of them were carrying bone spears. Others edged out from their caves. They slowly drew together, keeping close to the rocky cliff wall, and started talking in low, earnest tones.

They're puzzled, all right. Just play it cool. Don't make any sudden moves.

He leaned slightly forward and traced a triangle on the white sand with one finger.

When he looked up again, a grizzled, white-haired man had taken a step or two away from the conference group. Lee smiled at him and the elder froze in his tracks. With a shrug, Lee looked back at the first cave. The boy was still there, with a woman standing beside him, gripping his shoulder. Lee waved and smiled. The boy's hand fluttered momentarily, but he never got up the courage for a real wave.

The old man said something to the group, and one of the younger men stepped out to join him. Neither held a weapon. They walked to within a few meters of Lee, and the old man said something, as loudly and bravely as he could muster.

Lee bowed his head. "Good morning. I am Professor Sidney Lee of the University of Ottawa, which is one hell of a long way from here."

The old man and the younger one squatted down and started talking, both of them at once, pointing to the caves and then all around the beach and finally out to sea.

Lee held up his hands and said, "It ought to be clear to you that I'm from someplace else, and I don't speak your language. Now if you want to start teaching it to me . . ."

They shook their heads in a completely human way, talked to each other, said something else to Lee.

Lee smiled at them and waited for them to stop talking. When they did, he pointed to himself and said very clearly, "Lee."

He spent an hour at it, repeating only that one syllable, no matter what they said to him or to each other. The heat was getting fierce; Sirius was a blue flame searing his skin, baking the juices out of him.

The younger man got up and, with a shake of his head, spoke a few final words to the elder and then walked back to the group that still stood knotted by the base of the cliff. The old man rose, slowly and stiffly. He beckoned Lee to do the same.

As Lee got to his feet he saw the other men start to head out for the surf. A few boys followed behind, carrying several bone spears for their— what? Fathers? Older brothers?

As long as the spears are for the fish and not me, Lee thought.

The old man was saying something to him. Pointing toward the caves. He took a step in that direction, then motioned for Lee to come along. Lee hesitated. The old man smiled a toothless smile and repeated his invitation.

Grinning back at him in realization, Lee said aloud, "Okay, if you're not scared of me I guess I don't have to be scared of you."

It took more than a year before Lee learned their language well enough to understand roughly what they were saying. It was an odd language, sparse in some ways and almost completely devoid of pronouns.

His pronunciation of their words made the adults smile, when they thought he couldn't see them doing it. The children still giggled at his speech, but the old man—Ardraka—always scolded them when they did.

They called the planet Makta, and Lee saw to it that Rasmussen entered that as its official name in the expedition's log. He made a point of walking the beach alone one night each week, to talk with the others at the ship and make a personal report. He quickly found that most of what he saw, heard, and said inside the caves never got out to the relay transceiver buried up the beach; the cliff's rock walls were too much of a barrier.

Ardraka was the oldest of the clan, and the nominal chief. His son, Ardra, was the younger man who had also come out to talk to Lee on that first day. Ardra actually gave most of the orders. Ardraka could overrule him whenever he chose to, but he seldom exercised that right.

There were only forty-three people in the clan, nearly half of them elderly-looking. Eleven were pre-adolescent children; two of them infants. There were no obvious pregnancies. Ardraka must have been about fifty, judging by his oldest son's apparent age. But the old man had the wrinkled, sunken look of an eighty-year-old. The people themselves had very little idea of time beyond the basic rhythm of night and day. There were no seasons.

They came out of the caves only during the early morning and evening hours. The blazing midday heat of Sirius was too much for them to face. They ate crustaceans and the small fish that dwelled in the shallows along the beach, insects, and the grubby vegetation that clung to the base of the cliffs. Occasionally they found a large fish that had blundered into the shallows; then they feasted.

They had no wood, no metal, no fire. Their only tools were from the previous bones of the rare big fish, and hand-worked rock.

They died of disease and injury, they aged prematurely from malnutrition. They had to search constantly for food, especially since half their day was taken away from them by Sirius' blowtorch heat. They were more apt to be prowling the beach at night, hunting seaworms and crabs, than by daylight. *Grote and I damned near blundered right into them*, Lee realized after watching a few of the night gathering sessions.

There were some dangers. One morning he was watching one of the teen-age boys, a good swimmer, venture out past the shallows in search of fish. A shark-like creature found him first.

When he screamed, half a dozen men grabbed spears and dove into the surf. Lee found himself dashing into the water alongside them, empty-handed. He swam out to the youngster, already dead, sprawled face down in the water, half of him gone, blood staining the swells. Lee helped to pull the remains back to shore.

There wasn't anything definite, no one said a word to him about it, but their attitude toward him changed. He was fully accepted now. He hadn't saved the boy's life, hadn't shown any uncommon bravery. But he had shared a danger with them, and a sorrow.

Wheel the horse inside the gates of Troy, Lee said to himself. *Nobody ever warned you to beware of Earthmen bearing gifts*.

After he got to really understand their language, Lee found that Ardraka often singled him out for long talks. It was almost funny. There was something that the old man was fishing for, just as Lee was trying to learn where these people *really* came from.

They were sitting in the cool darkness of the

central cave, deep inside the cliff. All the outer caves channeled back to this single large chamber, high-roofed and moss-covered, its rocks faintly phosphorescent. It was big enough to hold four or five times the clan's present number without crowding.

It was midday. Most of the people were sleeping. A few of the children, off to the rear of the cave, were scratching pictures with pointed, fist-sized rocks on the packed bare earth back there. Lee sat with his back resting against a cool stone wall. The sleepers were paired off, man and mate, for the most part. The unmated adolescents slept apart. The older couples paired permanently, although the teens played the game as freely as they could.

Ardraka was lying beside him, eyes closed. Lee settled back and tried to turn off his thoughts, but the old man asked softly:

"Lee is not asleep?"

"No, Lee is not," he answered.

"Ardraka has seen that Lee seldom sleeps," Ardraka said.

"That is true."

"Is it that Lee does not need sleep as Ardraka does?"

Lee shook his head. "No, Lee needs sleep as much as Ardraka or any man."

"This . . . place . . . that Lee comes from. Lee says it is beyond the sea?"

"Yes, far beyond."

In the faint light of the gleaming rocks, the old man's heavy-boned, wrinkled face looked troubled, deep in difficult thought.

"Are there men and women living in Lee's place, men and women such as the people here?"

Lee nodded.

"And how did Lee come here? Did Lee swim across the sea?"

They had been through this a hundred times. "Lee came around the edge of the sea, walking on land just as Ardraka would."

Laughing softly, the old man said, "Ardraka is too feeble now for such a walk. Ardra could make such a walk."

"Yes, Ardra could."

"Ardraka has tried to dream of Lee's place and Lee's people. But such dreams do not come."

"Dreams are hard to command," Lee said.

"Yes, truly."

"And what of Ardraka and the people here?" Lee asked. "Is this the only place where such men and women live?"

"Yes. It is the best place to live. All other places are death."

"There are no men and women such as Ardraka and the people here living in another place?"

The old man thought hard a moment, then smiled a toothless smile. "Surely Lee jokes. Lee knows that Lee's people live in another place."

We've been around this bush before. Trying

another tack, he asked, "Have Ardraka's people always lived in this place? Did Ardraka's father live here?"

"Yes, of course."

"And Ardraka's father's father?"

A nod.

"And all the fathers, from the beginning of the people? All lived here, always?"

A shrug. "No man knows."

"Have there always been this many people living here?" Lee asked. "Did Ardraka's people ever fill this cave when the people slept here?"

"Oh, yes. . . . When Ardraka was a boy, many men and women slept in the outer caves, since there was no room for such men and women here. And when Ardraka's father was young, men and women even slept in the lower caves."

"Lower caves?"

Ardraka nodded. "Below this one, deeper inside the ground. No man or woman has been in the lower caves since Ardraka became chief."

"Why is that?"

The old man evaded Lee's eyes. "They are not needed."

"May Lee visit the lower caves?"

"Perhaps," Ardraka said. After a moment's thought, he added, "Children have been born and grown to manhood and died since any man set foot in the lower caves. Perhaps the lower caves are gone now. Perhaps Ardraka does not remember how to find them.''

"Lee would like to see the lower caves.''

Late that night he walked the beach alone, under the glowing star-poor sky, giving his weekly report back to the ship.

"He's being cagy about the lower caves,'' Lee said as the outstretched fingers of surf curled around his ankles.

"Why should he be so cautious?'' It was Marlene's voice. She was taking the report this night.

"Because he's no fool, that's why. These people have never seen a stranger before . . . not for generations, at least. Therefore their behavior toward me is original, not instinctive. If he's leery of showing me the caves, it's for some reason that's fresh in his mind, not some hoary tribal taboo.''

"Then what do you intend to do?''

"I'm not sure yet. . . .'' Lee turned to head back down the beach and saw Ardra standing twenty paces behind him.

"Company,'' he whispered. "Talk to you later. Keep listening.''

Ardra advanced toward him, and Lee couldn't help feeling the alienness of the young man's face, the bunched muscles in his shoulders and arms, the heavy brows that hid the expression in his eyes.

Ardraka's son said, "Many nights Ardra has seen Lee leave the cave and walk on the beach. Tonight Lee was talking, but Lee was alone. Does Lee speak to a man or woman that Ardra cannot see?"

His tone was flat, factual, neither frightened nor puzzled. If anything, menacing.

"Lee is alone," he answered as calmly as he could. "There is no man or woman here with Lee. Except Ardra."

"But Lee speaks and is silent. Then Lee speaks again."

He knows a conversation when he hears one, even if it's only one side of it and in a strange language.

Ardra suggested, "Perhaps Lee speaks to men and women from Lee's place, far beyond the sea?"

"Does Ardra believe that Lee can speak to men and women far away from this place?"

"Ardra believes that is what Lee does at night on the beach. Lee speaks with the *Karta*."

"*Karta?* What is the meaning of Karta?"

"It is an ancient word. It means men and women who live in another place."

Others, Lee translated to himself. "Yes," he said to Ardra. "Lee speaks to the Others."

Ardra's breath seemed to catch momentarily, then he said with deliberate care, "Lee speaks with the Others." His voice had an edge of steel to it now.

What have I stepped into?

"It is time to be sleeping, not walking on the beach," Ardra said in a tone that Lee knew was a command. And he started walking back toward the caves.

Thin as he was, Lee outweighed the chief's son by a few kilos, and was some ten centimeters taller. But he had seen the speed and strength in Ardra's stocky frame, and knew the difference in reaction time that the age difference between them made. So he didn't run or fight; he followed Ardra back to the caves and obediently went to sleep. Ardra stayed awake over him.

The next morning, when the men went out to fish and the women to gather greens and insects, Ardra took Lee's arm and led him to the back of the central cave. Ardraka and five other elders were waiting for him. They all looked very grim. Only then did Lee realize that Ardra was carrying a spear in his other hand.

They were sitting in a ragged semicircle, their backs to what looked like a tunnel entrance, their eyes hard on Lee. He sat at their focus, with Ardra squatting beside him.

"Lee," Ardraka began without preliminaries, "why is it that Lee wishes to see the lower caves?"

The question caught him by surprise. "Because . . . Lee wishes to learn more about Ardraka's people. Lee comes from far away, and knows little of Ardraka's father and the fathers of all the men and women here.''

"Is it true," one of the elders asked in an age-trembling voice, "that Lee speaks at night with the Others?" His inflection made the word sound special, fearful, ominous.

"Lee speaks to the men and women of the place where Lee comes from. It is like the way Ardraka speaks to Ardraka's grandfather . . . in a dream.''

"But Ardraka sleeps when doing such a thing. Lee is awake.''

Ardra broke in, "Lee says Lee's people live beyond the sea. Beyond the sea is the sky. Do Lee's people live in the sky?''

Off the edge of the world, just like Columbus.

"Yes," he admitted. "Lee's people come from the sky . . .''

"'See!'' Ardra shouted. "Lee is of the Others!''

The councilmen physically backed away from him. Even Ardraka seemed shaken.

"Lee is of the Others," Ardra repeated. "Lee must be killed before he kills Ardraka's people!''

"Kill?" Lee felt stunned. He had never heard any of them speak of violence before. "Why should Lee kill the people here?''

They were all babbling at once. Ardraka raised his hand for silence.

"To kill a man is very serious," he said painfully. "It is not certain that Lee is of the Others . . .''

"Lee says it with Lee's own mouth!'' Ardra

insisted. "Why else did Lee come here? Why does Lee want to see the lower caves?"

Ardraka glowered at his son, and the younger man stopped. "The council must be certain before acting."

Struggling to keep his voice calm, Ardra ticked off points on his stubby fingers: "Lee says Lee's people live in the sky . . . the Others live in the sky. Lee wishes to see the lower caves. Why? To see if more of Ardraka's people are there, so that Lee can kill *all* the people!"

The council members murmured and glanced at him fearfully. *Starting to look like a lynch jury.*

"Wait," Lee said. "There is more to the truth than what Ardra says. Lee's people live in the sky . . . that is true. But that does not mean that Lee's people are the Others. The sky is wide and large . . . wider even than the sea, by far. Many different people can live in the sky."

Ardraka's brows were knitted in concentration. "But Lee, if both Lee's people and the Others live in the sky, why have not the Others destroyed Lee's people as the Others destroyed Ardraka's ancestors?"

Lee felt his stomach drop away from him. *So that's it!*

"Yes," one of the councilmen said. "The Others live far from this land, yet the Others came here and destroyed Ardraka's forefathers and all the works of such men and women."

"Tell Lee what happened," he said, stalling for time to work up answers. "Lee knows nothing about the Others." *Not from your side of the war, at least.*

Ardraka glanced around at the council members sitting on both sides of him. They looked uncertain, wary, still afraid. Ardra, beside Lee, had the fixed glare of a born prosecutor. And the spear rested on the ground beside him.

"Lee is not of Ardraka's people," Ardra said, barely controlling the fury in his voice. "Lee must be of the Others. There are no people except Ardraka's people and the Others!"

"Perhaps that is not so," Ardraka said. "True, Ardraka has always thought it to be this way, but Lee looks like an ordinary man, not like the Others."

Ardra huffed. "No living man has seen the Others. How can Ardraka say——"

"Because Ardraka has seen pictures of the Others," the chief said quietly.

"Pictures?" They were all startled.

"Yes. In the deepest caves, where only the chief can go . . . and the chief's son. Ardraka has thought for a long time that soon Ardra should see the deepest cave. But no longer. Ardra must see the cave now."

The old man got up, stiffly, to his feet. His son was visibly trembling with eagerness.

"May Lee also see the pictures?" Lee asked.

They all began to protest, but Ardraka said firmly, "Lee has been accused of being of the Others. Lee stands in peril of death. It is right that Lee should see the pictures."

The council members muttered among themselves. Ardra glowered, then bent down and picked up the spear he had left at his feet. Lee smiled grimly to himself. *If those pictures give you the slightest excuse, you're going to ram that thing through me. The ideal lawman; sheriff, jury, and executioner.*

Far from having forgotten his way to the deeper caves, Ardraka threaded through a honeycomb of tunnels and chambers, always picking the path that slanted downward. Lee sensed they were spiraling deeper and deeper into the solid rock of the cliffs, far below sea level. The walls were crusted and a thick mat of dust clung to the ground, but everything shone with the same faint greenish luminosity as the upper caves. And beneath the dust the footing began to feel more like pitted metal than rock.

Finally Ardraka stopped. They were standing in the entryway to a fairly small chamber. The lighting was very dim. Lee stood behind Ardraka, and felt Ardra's breath on his neck.

"This is the place," Ardraka said solemnly. His voice echoed slightly.

They slowly entered the chamber. Ardraka walked to the farthest wall and wordlessly pointed to a jumble of lines scrawled at about eye level. The chamber was dark, but the lines of the drawing glowed slightly brighter than the wall itself.

Gradually, Lee pieced the picture together. It was crude, so crude that it was hard to understand. But there were stick figures of men that seemed to be running, hands raised over their heads protectively, and rough outlines of what might have been buildings with curls of smoke rising from them. Above them all were circular things, ships, with dots for ports. Harsh, jagged lines were streaking from the ships toward the stick figures and buildings.

"Men and women," Ardra said in a reverent whisper as he pointed to the stick drawings. "The men and women of the time of Ardraka's farthest ancestors. And *here*," his hand flashed to the circles, "are the Others."

Even in the dim light, Lee could see Ardra's face gaping at the picture. "The Others," he said, his voice barely audible.

"Look at Lee," Ardraka commanded his son. "Does Lee look like the Others, or like a man?"

Ardra seemed about to crumble. He said shakily, "Lee . . . Ardra has misjudged Lee. . . . Ardra is . . . ashamed."

"There is no shame," Lee said. "Ardra has done no harm. Ardra was trying to protect Ardraka's people." *And besides, you were right.*

Turning to Ardraka, Lee asked, "Is this all that you know of the Others?"

"Ardraka knows that the Others killed the people of Ardraka's forefathers. Before the Others came, Ardraka's ancestors lived in splendor: the living places covered the land everywhere; men and women swam the seas without fear of any creature of the deeps; men and women leaped through the sky and laughed at the winds and storms; every day was bright and good and there was no night. Then the Others came and destroyed all. The Others turned the sky to fire, and brought night. Only the people in the deepest caves survived. This was the deepest cave. Only the ancestors of Ardraka escaped the Others."

We destroyed this world, Lee told himself. *An interstellar war, aeons ago. We destroyed each other, old man. Only you've been destroyed for good, and we climbed back.*

Lee felt the weight of those aeons on him. *Sweet Christ Almighty, we did this to you.*

"Come," Ardraka said. "No more can be learned here. This place is dead. As dead as the people who made the pictures."

In the darkness, Lee nodded. As he turned back toward the entryway, his eyes caught a glint of something high up on the wall. He stopped momentarily and tried to make out what it was. But Ardra was right behind him, so he said nothing and followed Ardraka back up toward the harsh daylight.

It was a week before he dared to stroll on the

beach at night again, a week of torment, even though Ardra never gave him the slightest reason to think that he was still under suspicion.

The people at the ship were just as stunned as he was when he told them about it.

"We killed them," he whispered savagely at them, back in the comfort of the ship. "We destroyed them. We made the Pup explode to wipe them out completely."

"That's . . . farfetched," Rassmussen answered. But his voice sounded lame.

"What do we do now?" someone asked.

"There are other drawings on those walls," Lee said. "Too faint to see without lights."

"We should photograph the entire place."

"Yes, but how?"

Lee said, "I can take you down there, if we can put the whole clan to sleep for a few hours. Maybe gas . . ."

"That could work," Rassmussen agreed.

"A soporific gas?" Pascual's soft tenor rang incredulously in Lee's ears. "But we haven't the faintest idea of how it would affect them."

"It's the only way," Lee said. "You can't dig your way into those caves."

"But gas . . . it could kill them all."

"They're dead right now," Lee answered. "We killed them a long time ago. But we've still got to find where they originally came from. Before their relatives do the same job on us."

*   *   *

Lee slept less than ever the next few nights, and when he did he dreamed, but no longer about the buildings on Titan. Now he dreamed of the ships of an ancient Earth, huge round ships that spat fire on cities and roasted people as they ran. He dreamed of the Pup exploding and showering the planet with fire, blowing off the atmosphere, boiling the oceans, turning mountains into slag, killing every living thing on the surface of the planet, leaving a world bathed in a steam cloud, its ground ruptured with angry new volcanoes. Making hell out of heaven.

It was a rainy dark night when you could hardly see ten meters beyond the cave's mouth that they came. Lee heard their voices in his head as they drove the skimmer up onto the beach and clambered down from it and headed for the caves. Inside the caves, the people were asleep, sprawled innocently on the damp, musty ground.

Lee watched them sleeping unguarded as he listened to the voices of Grote and the rest of them, approaching. He stepped out to the cave's entrance and shuddered at the touch of the cold rain.

Out of the darkness a huge, bulky metal shape materialized, walking with exaggerated caution.

"Hello, Sid," Jerry Grote's voice said in his head, and the white metal shape raised a hand in greeting.

The Others, Lee thought as he watched four more powersuited figures appear in the dark rain.

He stepped out of the cave and let the rain wash over him, cold and numbing.

Grote hitched a gauntleted thumb at one of the others. "Pascual's got the gas. He's insisting on administering it himself."

Lee nodded. "I'll help. We've got to get it done quickly, without waking anybody. Who else is here?"

"Chien, Tanaka, and Stek."

"All right. Carlos, let's get going with the gas."

In the darkness, Lee couldn't make out the faces inside the powersuit helmets. Pascual and another who identified himself as Tanaka went into the caves with Lee. They spent more than an hour administering the gentlest soporific that the two medical men could concoct. Then more time as the doctors checked the physical reactions on each of the unconscious bodies that sprawled across the musty cave floor.

Finally Lee, Grote, and Stek headed for the lower caves. Even with the suit lamps to light the corridors, it was hard to retrace his steps down to the lowest level of the ancient shelter. But when they got to the bottommost chamber, Lee heard Stek break into a string of Polish exultation as he played his helmet lamp on the etched walls.

"Star maps!" the physicist said at last. "These are star maps, etched into the walls . . . as decoration! Or maybe it was meant to be a class-room or a planetarium."

Lee barely heard him. He was staring at the crudely drawn stick figures and the spherical ships of the Others, scratched as if by children over the fine, precise astronomical charts that covered the metal walls.

Grote photographed every inch of the walls in multispectrum film while Stek applied a kitful of radiation counters, X-ray cameras, and other equipment that Lee didn't recognize to the walls, ceiling, and floor.

"You want to know where these people originally came from?" Stek asked as he repacked his equipment after hours of work. "If they came from somewhere other than this planet, the information on these walls could tell us."

Lee said nothing.

"That's what you wanted, isn't it?" Grote asked. Lee heard his radio voice, of course. "Now you'll find out whether you're right or wrong."

"Yeah," said Lee.

By the time they got back up to the main sleeping cave and out to the beach again, it was full daylight, hot and painfully glaring. After a few eye-watering minutes, Lee could make out their faces inside the plastic helmets. He went to Pascual and Tanaka.

"We'll have to keep them sleeping until almost

dawn tomorrow,'' he told them. "Otherwise they'll suspect that something unusual's happened.''

Pascual's face looked concerned. "We can do that without harming them, I suppose.''

"They'll be hungry when they wake up," Tanaka said.

Lee turned to Grote. "How about taking a skimmer out and stunning a couple of big fish and towing them back here to the shallows?''

Grinning, Grote replied, "Hardly be fair game with the equipment on the skimmer.'' He turned and trudged for the car.

"Wait," Stek called to him. "Give me a chance to get these tapes and films back into the skimmer and safely stowed away.'' The physicist started off after Grote.

"Sid," Pascual said gently, "I want you to come back with us. You need a thorough medical check——''

A warning flashed through Lee. "Medical?" he snapped. "Are you playing front man for Lehman?''

Pascual's eyes widened with surprise. "If you had a mirror, you'd see why I want to check you. You're breaking out in skin cancers.''

Instinctively, Lee held out his hands to look at them. Both hands and forearms were marked with a few tiny blisters. And there were more on his belly and legs.

"It's from overexposure to the ultraviolet in the

sunlight. Hatfield's skin-darkening didn't fully protect you.''

"Is it serious?''

"I can't tell without a full examination.''

Just like a doctor. "I can't leave now,'' Lee said. "I've got to be here when they wake up, and make sure that they don't suspect they've been visited by the . . . by us.''

"And if they do suspect?''

Lee shrugged. "That's something we ought to know, even if we can't do anything about it.''

"Won't it be dangerous for you?''

"I doubt it.''

Pascual shook his head. "You mustn't stay out in the open much longer. I won't be responsible for it.''

"Fine. Do you want me to sign a release form?''

Grote brought the skimmer back around sundown, with two good-sized fish that he splashed, still dazed, into the shallow water. The others got aboard the skimmer around midnight, and with a few final radioed calls of parting, they drove off the beach and out to sea.

No word from Marlene. Lee felt annoyed. Then, turning it on himself, *What did you expect? She doesn't owe you a damned thing.*

At dawn the people woke up. They looked and acted completely normal, as far as Lee could tell. It was one of the children who noticed the still-sluggish fish in a shallow pool just outside the line of breakers. Every man in the clan splashed out, spear in hand, to get them. They feasted happily that day.

The dream was confusing. Somehow the buildings of Titan and the exploding star got mixed together. Lee saw himself being chased by something vast and formless. Then he stood above the sleeping form of one of Adraka's people, curled peacefully on the ground. Lee drove a bone spear through the man. He writhed like a fish on the spear, then turned and smiled bloodily up at Lee. It was Ardraka.

"Sid!"

He snapped awake. It was dark, and the people were sleeping, full-bellied. He was slouched near one of the entryways to the main sleeping cave, at the mouth of a tunnel that led to the openings in the cliff wall.

"Sid, can you hear me?" Grote's radio voice.

"Yes." He whispered so low that he could only feel the vibration in his throat.

"I'm up on the beach about three kilometers from the relay unit. You've got to come back to the ship. Stek thinks he's figured out the star charts."

Wordlessly, silently, Lee got up and padded through the tunnel and out onto the beach. The night was clear and bright. Dawn would be coming in another hour, he judged. The sea was calm,

the wind a gentle crooning as it swept down off
the cliffs.

"Sid, did you hear what I said? Stek has the
computer programmed to locate the frame of reference that the star charts were drawn from. By the
time we get back to the ship, he'll have the aliens'
homeworld pinpointed."

"I'm on my way." He still whispered, and
turned to see if anyone was following him across
the sand.

Grote was inside the skimmer, in a biosuit. No
one else. He jabbered about Stek's work on the
charts all the way back to the ship.

Just before they arrived, Grote suggested, "Uh.
Sid, you *are* going to put on some coveralls, aren't
you?"

When they got back to the ship, Lee insisted on
seeing Stek before doing anything else. Unhappily,
Pascual sprayed a biosuit over his coveralls and,
still barefooted, Lee padded into the "insiders"
part of the ship.

Stek was in the computer room, pacing with
unconcealed impatience. He was a large, round,
florid man with thinning red hair and a slightly
crooked mouth that made his face look as if he
was sneering at you all the time.

"One of the charts shows the sky from Sirius,"
the physicist told Lee. "We've established that
much. But the other one, on the opposite wall, has
a completely different reference center. The com-

puter's checking out all the known star positions for a hundred parsecs' radius. If it's any one of those stars, we'll nail it.''

"That's a lot of stars, isn't it?"

Nodding, Stek answered, "A few hundred thousand. The computer would've finished the analysis before you got here, except that the chart is old—really old. Star positions have changed since the chart was drawn. For example, there's something that looks like the Big Dipper, but it's——''

Lee broke in, "Can you still find their home-world, even though the charts are ancient?"

Stek flushed momentarily. He didn't like to be interrupted. "Yes, of course . . . if there's enough astronomical data stored in the computer. We can backtrack and . . .''

"Suppose the computer doesn't have the data you need?"

"It does," Stek snapped. "I'm sure it does."

"But if it doesn't?"

"Then we'll have to wait until we get back to Earth.''

"When will we know?"

Looking grim, Stek replied, "I thought we'd have had an answer by now. Something must be wrong with the programming. I'll have to check it out.''

For the first time, Lee looked past the physicist's red-splotched face to the two unhappy crew members who had been pressed into programming the computer. They were sitting uneasily by the main input console, which flashed lights at them.

"I'll get the answer," Stek promised, almost savagely. "Just give me a few hours more."

Lee nodded, "Call me when you do."

He headed back for the "outsiders" globe, with Pascual at his shoulder, thinking, *We'll find their homeworld. Ardraka's homeworld. Ardraka's people are our enemy. Their brothers, the ones who built the machines on Titan, are still out there somewhere. Maybe searching for Ardraka and any other survivors. Maybe searching for us.*

Marlene was back at the Sirius globe. When he saw her, he wanted to take her and hold her and love her. He wanted to forget about homeworlds and wars and ancient enemies. But Pascual and all the other "outsiders" were right there with them, so he merely smiled at her and said hello as Pascual led him to the dispensary.

The six "outsiders" ate together after Lee's medical checkup, a sort of reunion meal, although Lee wasn't allowed to eat Earth food yet. There were the usual jokes about the terrible native foods.

Marlene said seriously, "You've lost so much weight, Sid."

"Ever see a fat Sirian?" He meant it as a joke; it came out waspish. She dropped the subject.

Lehman joined them, biosuited, after dinner. The six "outsiders" and the psychiatrist sat in the gallery area, trying to convince themselves they were relaxing over coffee and drinks. But Lee knew better.

"What's keeping Stek? He said he'd call when he had the job done."

Charnovsky rumbled, "He can't backtrack the positions of a hundred thousand stars over thousands of years. The computer, doesn't have the capacity . . . or the data storage."

"Then why doesn't he admit it?" Marlene asked. "Why keep everyone in suspense like this?"

"Stubbornness," Charnovsky answered.

Hatfield said, "I'm tenacious; he's stubborn."

Nobody laughed.

Lehman couldn't eat or drink anything with the biosuit on. He merely sat back calmly in a web chair and asked, "Do you really think we'll be able to find the homeworld of these people?"

"Of course," Charnovsky said. "But probably not until we return to Earth."

"Shouldn't we radio the information back to Earth? That way it'll get there in eight years, instead of thirty."

"Why do you think Stek is working so furiously?" Charnovsky countered. "Do you think he enjoys beating programmers with his tongue?"

"Well, frankly . . ." Doris started.

Charnovsky waved her silent. "No, our physicist wants to unravel the secret himself. He wants to solve the puzzle, get the glory. If he can't do it,

Rassmussen will beam the data to Earth and Stek's name will be no more than a footnote."

"Wouldn't you do the same thing, in his place?" Lehman asked.

"Of course! But there is one additional step I would take, to guarantee success."

"What's that?"

Charnovsky grinned hugely, "I would sabotage the radio transmitter."

Lee had to admit that Charnovsky would probably do just that.

While they were still laughing, Lehman turned to him, "And when we find where their homeworld is, what then?"

Their laughter died. Lee shrugged and answered, "I don't know. Maybe we go out and see if they're still there. Maybe we reopen the war."

"If there was a war," Marlene said.

"There was. It might still be going on, for all we know. Maybe we're still just a small part of it, a frontier skirmish."

"A skirmish that wiped out almost all the life on this planet?" Doris wondered.

"And almost wiped out Earth, too," Lee reminded her. And himself.

"But what about the people on this planet, Sid?" Lehman insisted. "What about the people in the caves?"

Lee couldn't answer.

"Do we let them die out, just because they

might have been our enemies a few millenia ago?"

"They'd still be our enemies, if they knew who we are," Lee said tightly.

"So we let them die?"

Lee tried to blot their faces out of his mind, to erase the memory of Ardraka and the children and Ardra apologizing shamefacedly and the people singing as they brought in a fish. . . .

"No," he heard himself say. "We've got to help them. They can't hurt us anymore, and God knows we've hurt them enough."

He looked up and saw Marlene smiling at him.

The viewscreen on the galley's far wall suddenly buzzed into life. Stek's face filled the screen: excited, flushed with exultation.

"I've got it! I've got it! Look!"

Somebody knocked a cup over as they turned to see the screen. It clattered to the floor unnoticed. They sat and stared at the screen.

It showed the etched-metal chart from the alien's underground chamber. Then the same chart, but this time on the computer's output screen. Where there had been dull metal and fine-worked symbolic stars of four or six points, now there was a scintillating holographic projection and the stars were represented by white pinpoints.

The stars began to move, shift across the field of view.

"I took the original chart and tried to use the computer's astronomical data storage to move the stars from their ancient positions as given on the chart to their present positions," Stek explained with some pomposity. Lee noticed that now it was *I* rather than the *we* he'd used when the problem was still unsolved.

"I tried about a thousand stars with no success at all. We'd always wind up with a completely unrecognizable pattern—which meant that we were on the wrong frame of reference."

The viewscreen still showed the poinpoints of light moving, drifting, leisurely, calmly, with stately deliberation.

"The proof of the pudding, of course," Stek went on, "is that when we hit on the right frame of reference, we'll see the stars in their present positions, just as we see them at night right now."

Lee watched, frozen still, as the star pattern slowly became recognizable. There was the Big Dipper all right, still a lopsided, but definitely there. And Orion. And . . .

The movement stopped. The stars hung in their places.

Stek said, "That's just how you'd see them right now. I found the original home star for these people."

"What is it?" somebody asked.

Stek's face reappeared in the screen. He was smiling and deadly serious at the same time.

"It's the sun," he said.

"The sun?"

Lee felt the breath puff out of him, as if some-one had hit him in the solar plexus.

"The sun?" they were babbling.

"Then they came from our solar system?"

"But how . . ."

"They came from Earth!"

"Jesus Christ! They *are* Neanderthals!"

Lee stood up. "They're from Earth!" he shouted. "They're part of us!"

"But how coud . . ."

"Neanderthals?"

"They were a colony of *ours*," Lee realized. "They're our brothers, not our enemies!"

"But they're Neanderthals."

"They're human, they're from Earth. We're not enemies. The Others were another race, somebody else . . . an enemy that nearly wiped us both out and smashed Earth's civilization. The Others built those damned machines on Titan, Ardraka's people didn't. And we didn't destroy this world . . . the Others did!"

"But that's . . ."

"How can you be sure?"

"He is right," Charnovsky said, his heavy bass rumbling through the other voices. They all stopped to hear him. "There are too many coincidences any other way. These people are completely human because they came from Earth. Any other explanation is extraneous. They are Neanderthal and we are Sapiens. Both are equally intelligent."

Lee grabbed the Russian by the shoulders. "Alex, we've got work to do! We've got to help them. We've got to introduce them to fire, and metals, and cereal grains . . ."

Charnovsky laughed. "Yes, yes, of course. But not tonight, eh? Tonight we celebrate."

"No," Lee said, realizing where he belonged. "Tonight I go back to them."

"Go back?" Marlene asked.

"Tonight I go back with a gift," Lee went on. "A gift from my people to Ardraka's. A plastic boat from the skimmer. That's a gift they'll be able to understand and use."

Lehman said, "You still don't know who built the machines on Titan."

"We'll find out."

"And we'll have to return to Earth before the next expedition can possibly get here."

"Some of us can wait here for the next expedition. I will, anyway."

Marlene didn't say anything, but he saw in her eyes the bitter pain of death. *I've lost her,* he realized.

With an ache of regret smoldering inside him, he turned to Lehman. "Would you ask Grote to take me back in the skimmer?"

Lehman glanced at Marlene, then nodded.

Lee went to her. "I've got to."

"I know," she said.

"Maybe . . ."

"What?"

He shook his head. "Nothing."

She looked at him for a long moment, then turned away.

The Earth was the same, yet completely changed. Sidney Lee finally returned from Sirius, years after the other members of the first expedition. He came back to a world of twenty billion strangers. The cities felt bigger, more crowded, colder than he had remembered them. The university was hauntingly different: buildings where he remembered groves of trees, a gymnasium where the off-campus bar used to be, unfamiliar names and faces who spoke in words and expressions that seemed almost right but not really.

Even the Training Center was busier, larger—and old. The trees were sturdy and mature now. The buildings had weathered. The lawns he remembered as newly seeded had more than a half-century of footpaths cut through rich, hardy grass.

And Marlene wasn't there.

They honored him. They gave him awards, they offered him endowed chairs with full tenure, they held banquets for him, they invited him to lecture. He traveled the world for more than a year telling them of what he had learned, showing them pictures of Ardraka (who had died just before Lee left the planet), of Ardra and the rest of the Neanderthals.

They argued with him. Wherever he went there were the debates, the clashes, the arguments. The bright young students listened to Lee's theories about the Others and the machines on Titan. The old professors—younger than Lee but more aged—watched his pictures and heard his words with fear plain on their faces.

All of anthropology was in ferment. Learned men turned their full wrath on Lee and his theories, fearful that their lifetimes of work would be washed away by a new chronology, a new ordering of the facts of human prehistory. Others, mostly the young, set out determinedly to find the evidence where it had always lain—in the earth.

When the evidence began to come in from the first diggings, those opposed to Lee turned to ridicule, to statistics, to any arguments they could find rather than rethink their professions. For a while Lee fought back, traded evidence for insult, insisting everywhere that the earlier views of man's ancestry and prehistory were mainly wrong, mistaken, based on scanty proof and pat assumptions.

But wherever he went, whoever he argued against, whatever support he received, nowhere could he find Marlene.

Finally very late one night, after a grueling battle with one of the world's most famous anthropologists and debaters, Lee stood on the tiny balcony outside his room in a prefab plastic chrome hotel room. The city spread out before him in the warm night was (he was sure) either Dresden or Pretoria. That night he looked into the sky and saw the stars for the first time since returning to Earth. Really saw them, looking down on him hard and eternal, the uncompromising conscience of the world. Then he remembered that his real work had just begun. He knew where he should be.

And he realized where she was, too.

7. RETURN TO TITAN

The shuttle settled slowly, descending from the dark sky of Titan on a tongue of plasma flame to the scarred landing shield.

Before the engines had shut down, a flexible loading tube wormed its way from the domed terminal building toward the shuttle rocket. Automatically it lifted and attached itself to the shuttle's airlock hatch.

Sidney Lee was the only passenger. He walked slowly through the tube, alone, carrying a single travel kit in one hand. The air here felt different, cooler, fresher, than the air in the shuttle. He sensed the frigid ammonia atmosphere just centimeters away, on the other side of the tube's thin plastic wall.

Someone had scrawled on a curving overhead structural beam: ABANDON ALL HOPE, YE WHO ENTER HERE.

Thanks, Lee said to himself.

The hatch at the other end of the tube opened automatically as Lee approached it. Standing on the other side of the hatch, inside the big empty dome of the terminal building, were three men: two youngsters and an old man who looked vaguely familiar.

"Dr. Lee," the old man said as he stepped forward and offered his hand, "I'm Kim Bennett. . . ."

Kim Bennett. Lee recalled a man his own age, quick, active, bright. The man in front of him was gray-eyed, stooped, wrinkled.

"Of course, Kim. I'm sorry . . . it's been a long time since . . ."

Bennett smiled wryly. "Dr. Lee, I'm afraid you're thinking of my father. He's the one who went to school with you. I'm Kimbal Bennett, Jr."

Lee felt his hand slip out of Bennett's grasp. "Oh," he said, feeling as stupid as he sounded.

"Dad died several years ago," Bennett went on, "before you returned from Sirius, I guess it was."

"I'm . . . I *am* sorry. . . ." Lee muttered.

Bennett dismissed the problem with a smile. Turning, he introduced the two younger men. "This is Dr. Monsel, and Dr. Aiken."

They shook hands with some solemnity. Monsel

was dark, deep-voiced, with a carefully trimmed beard. Aiken was golden-blond, chunky, pleasant-faced.

"I'll take your bag, Dr. Lee," Aiken said. "Did you have any other luggage? Any equipment?"

Lee had to smile at his solicitousness as he took the travel kit. "No, just this."

Monsel said, "The lift tube is this way." Extending his hand toward Lee, "Uh, you might find the low gee here a bit difficult for walking, Dr. Lee. . . ."

"The ship spun down to Titan gee on the way here," he answered. "They prepared me for it. And I *was* here before, you know."

Monsel's dark face reddened noticeably.

Bennett walked beside Lee, the two younger men slightly ahead of them, as they crossed the spacious dome. *Hasn't changed much,* Lee saw. The dome was mostly empty. A surface tractor was parked by the main airlock, across the worn plastisteel floor. Here by the smaller airlock there were the same lockers for pressure suits and equipment racks standing mutely. The four men were the only people in the dome.

As they walked toward the lift tube, on the farthest side of the dome away from the airlocks, Lee glanced up at the dome's clear top. Only a few stars shone through.

"Saturn's over behind us," Bennett said softly.

Lee turned and saw the fat gaudy curve of the

giant planet, yellow and ochre and flame-orange stripes and the razor-thin line of the rings. A circus tent planet, an impossibility, a clown that grinned down on them as they scrabbled around the towers that the Others had left.

"Um . . . the lift tube . . ." Bennett suggested gently.

They went down the tube, dropping with blurring speed from the surface dome toward the living and working quarters of the underground center. The lift compartment was exactly as Lee had remembered it, except for being older, more scarred from three generations of boots and crates and frustrations pounding the floors and walls, wearing them into a tired metallic dullness. Graffiti were scribbled on the walls:

The machines run on swamp gas.
Sam Khinovy has frostbite of the brain.
The eyes of Texas are looking the other way.

The lift still worked smoothly, though. Lee remembered across the years the particular whine of this lift's electrical motors. *Keep working for another five hundred centuries and you'll be half as good as the Others' machines.*

The whining stopped and the car eased to a halt and the doors slid open and Marlene was there. Lee felt a jolt of electricity flash through him.

She hadn't changed. Tall, slim, auburn hair, incredible deep brown eyes, everything about her was beautiful. She was wearing a black jumpsuit, long sleeves, turtleneck, stretchpants. A green scarf at her throat for a touch of color.

He heard himself croak, "Hi . . . hello."

"Sid, hello. How are you? I'm sorry I didn't get up to the dome to meet you, but I . . ."

"No, never mind. It's okay. How are you?"

He took her hand and held on to it and didn't hear a word she said as he just watched her, watched her face and looked to see what was in her eyes as they walked down the corridor together. He was dimly aware that the once pristine-white walls were now covered with handwriting, drawings, even some strikingly good full-color abstracts.

Abruptly they stopped in front of a numbered but nameless door set into the long, curving, graffiti-illustrated corridor. Lee suddenly realized that the three other men were still with them.

"This is your place," Bennett said. "I hope it's all right."

"It will be," Lee answered. "Don't worry about it."

Aiken said, "If there's anything wrong, or you need anything, you can call me."

"Fine, thanks."

Aiken handed him back his travel kit.

"Why don't you get yourself unpacked," Bennett suggested, "and then give me a call? Have dinner at my place. There ought to be some first-rate Scotch among the cargo the shuttle just brought in."

"Okay. Good."

Bennett turned to Marlene. "You too, I know you're not a Scotch drinker, but we can . . ."

She shook her head. "I can't. I'd like to, but I'm in the middle of a series of observations. I ought to be topside right now."

Lee stood there, feeling stupid and helpless, wishing they'd all stop being friendly and solicitous, wanting them to go away, all of them, except Marlene.

She said to him, "Honest, Sid, I'm really stretching it now to be here at all. These atmospheric tide observations have to be done. . . ."

"Sure," he said.

"I'll call you later," she said. And she turned and walked off down the corridor.

He watched her for a moment, then muttered some banalities at Bennett and the others and went inside.

His quarters were more spacious than his room had been the last time he was on Titan. There were three whole rooms, solid comfortable furniture, and wall-sized viewscreens in both the living room and bedroom. The smaller study had a desktop viewscreen.

Somebody had programmed the wall screens to show views of Earth. The living room seemed to look out on a green meadow, complete with butterflies and a spindly-legged colt frolicking on the brown of a grassy hill. The bedroom showed the jeweled lights of a city at night. Lee looked around briefly for a control switch to shut them off.

Finally he gave up, dropped his travel kit on the bed and punched the telephone button on the night table beside the bed.

"Get Marlene Ettinger, please," he said to the phone.

In a few seconds, the phone's contralto computer voice purred, "Miss Ettinger is not in her quarters."

Lee huffed. "I know. Find her."

He unzipped the travel kit and sprinkled its contents over the bed. The big viewscreen's cityscape vanished and Marlene's face filled the wall. Lee sank down onto the bed.

"Oh, Sid. It's you."

She was already in a pressure suit, he could see. Only the helmet wasn't on yet.

Suddenly he wasn't sure of what he wanted to say. "Marlene . . . I can skip this dinner with Bennett. Why don't you call me when you're finished?"

She shook her head and answered seriously, "I'm not sure how long this will take, Sid. And there's a mountain of work for me to do. I've really got to run. I'll call you tomorrow. All right?"

He shrugged. "Tomorrow."

The screen went blank. Lee found that he was staring at it anyway. With an effort, he turned away.

*   *   *

Bennett's apartment was even bigger than Lee's, but then the older man (*born forty years after I was*, Lee said to himself) had a wife and several Persian cats.

They had a polite cocktail before dinner. Lee had forgotten the languid, slow-motion fall of liquids under Titan's low gravity. You could spill a drink and then scoop it up in your glass before it hit the floor, if you were fast enough. Through the meal, Lee moved and talked mechanically, his mind on Marlene. After dinner Mrs. Bennett disappeared into another room while Lee and this younger-older man who looked like his classmate tried to relax over more Scotch.

Lee slouched on the sofa, trying to at least look comfortable, while Bennett sat in a contour chair facing him.

"The living quarters have changed a lot since the last time I was here," Lee said, carefully trying to avoid references to time and age. "They're absolutely luxurious now."

Bennett smiled sadly. "Of course. Well, why shouldn't they be luxurious? When you were here last time this was a frontier outpost. Now it's a museum."

"A museum? What do you mean?"

The gray-haired man took a sip of Scotch before replying. "No one here has done any significant scientific work on the machines in years. We're just caretakers."

"How can . . . but . . . I thought there was a lot of work going on here."

"There is," Bennett said. "Things like Marlene's atmospheric tides measurements. Good work, too. But it's got nothing to do with the machines."

Lee could feel his forehead wrinkling into a frown. "I don't understand."

"The machines have beaten us," Bennett answered softly. "We'll never understand them. Most of the permanent staff here is starting to look on them as religious totems, almost. They're awed. I don't blame them; so am I."

"You're not serious. . . ."

Leaning forward and tapping a finger on Lee's leg, Bennett said with quiet intensity, "It's been just about seventy-five years since the machines were discovered, and we've gotten nowhere with them. I've spent my whole *life* here. I was *born* here on Titan. In three weeks I'm retiring and going Earthside. I'm through."

Lee said nothing.

"That's why I was so glad to learn that you were coming back here. I want you to take over my position. I'm supposed to be the head of the scientific staff here, but the job has amounted to nothing more than paper-shuffling."

"I can't step in cold and . . ."

"Of course you can. The director has already approved it."

"But what about the people who've been working with you? The people who've been here for years? They'll resent having me step in.''

Bennett smiled again, but this time with real pleasure. ''Didn't you see the respect those two kids had for you this afternoon? You're famous: the man who first deciphered the Martian script, who found the Neanderthals on Sirius.''

''But . . .''

''Listen,'' Bennett insisted. ''I'm asking you to take over a frustrating, maddening position. But I've done you one important favor. I've stocked the scientific staff here with as many eager youngsters as I could. I've spent the last year, ever since you returned from Sirius, cleaning out as much of the deadwood as I could. I was hoping you'd come back. I think you'll find the best staff we've had here in a generation. And they—most of them, at least—they'll look up to you. You're a big man on this campus.''

Shaking his head, Lee said, ''No, I'm the man who cracked up the last time he was here. That's one reason why I came back—to see if I can really face those machines again.''

''You will; don't worry about it.''

''I'm not that sure. . . .''

''Listen, there's something here that's far worse than the machines. It's the director we've got now—Charles Peary. He's an ass. An ass with power. He sees his duty as protecting the machines from any scientific workers who might get finger smudges on them. He's beaten many a good man down into a blubbering lump of frustration. All he wants to do is to sit here and collect his pay and turn the machines into a tourist attraction for religious pilgrims . . . and government officials.''

Lee stared at the older man. ''But you can't let him get away with that!''

Again Bennett smiled sadly, ''I'm too old to fight him. And for all I know, he might be right. Maybe the machines *are* simply beyond our capacity to understand.''

''No!''

Shrugging, Bennett said, ''All right. But I know this much: they're beyond my capacity. I'm tired. I want to go back to Earth and find a quiet island someplace and spend the rest of my life soaking up the sun.''

After a minute's thought, Lee said, ''I guess I'd better meet the director, then. What'd you say his name was?''

''Peary. Charles Peary.''

That night, back in his own bedroom, while a phosphorescent waterfall cascaded down the viewscreen wall, Lee tried to reach Marlene again. The phone's slightly sultry voice told him: ''Miss Ettinger is occupied in experimental work topside at present and is not to be disturbed. If this is an emergency, however . . .''

''No, it's not an emergency.'' *Just life and death.*

His bed, Lee found, had a fluid mattress. In Titan's low gravity, such comfort was absolutely decadent.

The first thing he did on awakening was to call Marlene. The viewscreen stayed blank but she answered sleepily, "Who is it?"

"Oh hell," he said, "I woke you up."

"Sid? Hi. Yes, you did. We had some late runs with the computer last night . . ."

He felt awkwardly foolish. "I'm sorry, Marlene. Go back to sleep."

"No, it's all right. . . . I had to get up soon anyway. Excuse the blank screen, will you? I'm not decent."

"Sure. Look, can we get together for lunch? I want to talk with you."

"Lunch? Okay. What time?"

"Noon . . . twelve thirty. You name it."

"Uh . . . better make it late. Thirteen hundred?"

"Fine. Is the cafeteria still in the same place?"

"Oh no," her voice answered. "Everything's been changed around since you were here. But it's easy to find. Just follow the yellow markers in the corridors. Or ask anybody."

"Okay. See you at thirteen hundred."

"Fine."

"Throttled down to zero?" The director's voice sounded wounded. "But that's just not true, Dr.

Lee. We're accomplishing some very fine and important work here.''

He was a sizable man who somehow gave the impression of smallness. His build was on the burly side, except that he seemed to be going soft, portly middle, flabby face largely hidden behind a shaggy mouse-gray beard. Hair thinning, eyes watery blue, voice soft with a slight drawling accent.

''Why, we've made important strides in planetary physics over the past few years. Why, right now we've got a team of people doing fine work on atmospheric tides. And as soon as we can get our requisitions through the Earthside red-tape mill, we'll get the computers we need for a first-class eqrthquake prediction center.''

He leaned back in his desk chair and folded his hands over his middle with a *what-do-you-think-of-that* expression. Sitting across the desk from the director, Lee replied, ''But the alien buildings, the machines . . . what's being done about them?''

Peary's self-satisfied smile evaporated. He leaned forward and placed his chunky forearms on the desktop. ''That's a different matter. An entirely different matter. We're in a caretaker stage there.''

''A what?''

''Caretaker stage. No further direct investigations of the machinery are possible without physical damage being done to the machines. Naturally, we can't risk that, so . . .''

''Can't risk damaging the machines?''

"Of course not."

Lee thought a moment. Then, "Mr. Peary . . ."

"Please call me Charles."

"All right—Charles. Are you really certain that no useful work can be done on the machines without damaging them?"

Peary's shaggy face took on a look of regret. "You scientists have been poking around those machines for three generations and more. Nothing's been discovered. Bennett admitted to me years ago that the only useful thing he could think of was to crack 'em open and see what makes 'em tick. Well now, regulations specifically state that nothing is to be done that might interfere with the continued operation of those machines. Those are the rules. I don't make 'em, I just carry them out."

"But . . ."

"No sense arguing; there's nothing I can do about it."

"I was going to say," Lee countered firmly, "that if I can show you a useful line of investigation that doesn't require destroying any of the machinery, will you let us carry it out?"

"Well now, I don't think you can, frankly."

"But if I do."

"I'll have to judge the idea on its own merits. I can't commit myself to a judgment ahead of time."

Getting cagey. "Okay, fine. That's all I ask." Lee started to get out of his chair.

"I don't think you can come up with anything

that hasn't been tried already," Peary said. "No reflection on you, understand."

Lee looked down at him. "Sure. I understand." He turned and walked to the door of the office.

"Doubt you could damage the machines anyway," he heard Peary mutter, "even if you try."

Lee found the cafeteria, after a half-hour search through the graffiti-covered corridors. One of the scrawled lines, just before the cafeteria itself, read:

Food for thought, si.
Food for stomach, no!

The cafeteria was much bigger and more comfortable than the cramped collection of tables and chairs that he remembered from long ago. And it was quiet, despite the crowd eating, talking, moving through the spacious room. *Acoustical dampers,* Lee realized. One entire wall was a giant viewscreen which, at the moment, was showing skiers sleeking down an Earthly hillside, trailing plumes of sparkling powdery snow. No one even looked at it.

Marlene was already at a table, Lee saw, with another man: young-looking, crew-cut, athletically trim, smiling and gesturing expressively for her. Lee punched buttons on the food selector wall as quickly as he could, waited an endless twenty seconds for his food tray to pop out of the slot at the end of the selector panel, then hurried to join them.

". . . and after you've exhausted yourself on

the slopes all day, they give you this huge dinner and a ton of wine, and they still expect you to dance half the night and . . ."

Marlene looked up as Lee put his tray on the table next to her.

"Hello, Sid. Have you met Marty Richards?"

"No. How are you?"

Richards lifted his tail a few centimeters off his chair and took Lee's hand in a strong grip. His smile was dazzling.

"Hi. I'm with the physics group."

"Marty's head of the physics section," Marlene corrected as Lee sat down.

"That's pretty good for somebody your age. Or have you been on a star mission?"

Richards grinned some more and shook his head. "No, but I'd sure like to do that sometime. Maybe I'll put in for a star flight when the next round of them comes up. We're sure not accomplishing much around here."

Lee peeled the foil off his tray and found that he had two containers of soup and no salad.

"Marty was telling me about the skiing in Argentina," Marlene said.

Lee asked, "Why aren't you accomplishing much here?"

"We're not allowed to," Richards answered immediately. "I've got half a dozen projects that I've suggested to Bennett. They're all sitting on his desk. Or Peary's. None of them have been okayed."

"I talked with Peary this morning. He agreed to okay projects that don't involve tampering with the machines."

Richards shrugged. "So what's new? There's not much we can do that doesn't tamper with the machines in one way or another. I mean, they've been photographed and analyzed all through the electromagnetic spectrum down to gamma ray probes. We've done all the passive things you can think of. A hundred different ways and a thousand different times."

"Then think of something else."

Richards laughed.

"Listen to me," Lee snapped. "I want to see you people *working*, and working inside those buildings, not on planetary physics."

Richards stopped and stared at him. Then, "*You* want?"

"That's right. I'm taking Bennett's place. He's leaving."

"Kim's leaving? After all the years he's put in . . . I guess we should have expected it."

Lee said nothing.

"So you're going to start taking things seriously again. You want us to get to work on the machines."

"Right. That's what we're here for."

"What about Peary?"

"I'll take care of him. He's my responsibility."

Marlene said, "Sid, be careful of Peary. He's insidious. He'll smile at you and agree with you, and then when your back is turned he'll renege on everything he's told you."

"Okay. We'll just have to keep watching him. And maybe we can learn how to operate when *his* back is turned."

Richards gaped at him. "You mean that?"

"Hell, yes."

Richards' grin started to take on the aspect of a canary-fed cat. "Okay . . . let me have a couple of sessions with my people. There are some damned good ideas moldering in the dust around here. Maybe we can resurrect them."

"Good. Do that."

They finished eating and Richards excused himself from the table.

"Suddenly you're giving orders," Marlene said.

Lee nodded. "I'd like to give you some orders too."

"I'm only an atmospheric physicist. I can't do anything about the buildings."

"That's not what I had in mind."

She rested her elbows on the table and leaned slightly toward him. "You've changed, Sid. You're positively aggressive."

"I've learned," he said. "I've found what I want; now I have to get it."

A smile flickered on her lips. A sad smile. "Sid

. . . I had to work awfully hard to get over you. You really built a wall around yourself and shut me out.''

"I know. I wish I could make that wall disappear. I want to. Maybe . . . maybe together we can break it down.''

She said nothing.

"You look awfully damned serious," he said.

"So do you."

"Well, I'll tell you one thing. When I saw you sitting here listening to that young twirp, batting those lovely eyes at him . . .''

"I was *not* batting my eyes!''

"Oh no?"

She giggled. "No, I wasn't . . . not consciously, at any rate.''

"Consciously or unconsciously . . . when I saw you two together, that sure as hell put a dent in any walls I've got around me.''

"Maybe there's hope for you yet.''

"Maybe there's hope for us.''

Her face completely serious again, her voice so low he could barely hear it, "You're not the only one who's been hurt, you know.''

"I know. And I'm sorry. Can we start over?''

"We can try.''

"That's all I ask.''

"No promises, though. No commitments.''

"Yeah.''

*　　*　　*

Lee spent the afternoon going through the underground center, poking into laboratories and workshops, meeting people. He knew Charnovsky was on Titan but couldn't locate him. Pascual was in the infirmary, taking care of a wardful of children who were being tested for allergies and immunities.

"In a closed-in environment like this, we must be extremely careful about infectious diseases," the brown-skinned doctor said in his soft voice as he and Lee walked back toward Pascual's office. The corridors in the infirmary area were hospital white and spotlessly clean of graffiti.

"It's a regular city now, isn't it?" Lee asked rhetorically. "Schools, hospital, everything. How long do people stay here?"

Pascual said, "The scientific staff comes and goes; you know, a scientist will be here for two or three years, on the average. I've been here a year and a half myself. In six months I'll be leaving. But the others, the administrators like Bennett and Peary and the non-technical staff—most of them have been here for a long time. They're permanently settled here, whether they realize it or not."

"How long has Peary been here?"

Pascual shrugged. "I'm not sure. We could look it up. I think two of his children were born here, and the youngest is six."

"H'mm."

"You know that Charnovsky is here? He arrived a few months ago."

"Yes, I've been trying to find him. He's probably up topside, trying to dig rocks up from underneath the ice. Anybody else from the Sirius crew?"

"No . . . oh, yes, of course. Lehman. I haven't seen him yet, maybe he's not even arrived. But I saw his name on the list of new arrivals yesterday. Right under your name, as a matter of fact."

Naturally, Lee thought.

So Lee invited the Sirius people to his place for dinner that night: Marlene, Pascual, and Charnovsky. It was a quiet gathering. Marlene insisted on taking care of the cooking, although Lee had nothing but pre-cooked meals for them. Charnovsky looked tired; he had been out topside for several days. They asked Lee about the Neanderthals and were appropriately sympathetic when he told them that Ardraka had died. They broke up early and Lee walked Marlene back to her quarters. He kissed her goodnight. She didn't invite him in and he didn't insist. He walked back to his place and finished a nearly dead bottle of cognac before trying to sleep.

Two days later, Bennett called a meeting of all the scientific department heads. Charnovsky was there, and Richards, and four others whom Lee had briefly met during his tours through the underground settlement.

They sat at an oval table in a small conference

room. Bennett was the only old man among them. The others were all younger: either star-young, like Lee and Charnovsky, or truly youthful, like the rest of them.

Bennett stood at the head of the table, with Lee sitting beside him.

"I suppose you all know by now," he said, "that I've decided to leave. Dr. Lee has accepted my request that he take over in my place." He turned to Lee. "Sid, I suppose that's all the ritual we need. The floor is yours."

A little surprised, Lee got up from his chair and looked them over. They shifted uneasily in their seats, feet scraped the plastic flooring. Somebody coughed nervously.

"I've only been here a few days," Lee began, "and had no idea that Kim wanted to sandbag me into taking his job while he strolled off for the South Sea Isles. . . ."

A few polite chuckles.

"But in the short time I've been here, it's become abundantly clear to me that the scientific staff is being hamstrung by regulations and restrictions on what we can do. I hope to put an end to that."

They stirred in their chairs, but now there was an edge of tenseness in it, expectancy.

"Now, I don't mean that we're going to charge into the buildings up there and tear them apart. I agree that we shouldn't tinker with them until we have some idea of what we're doing. But neither do I believe that there's nothing we can do. I want you to tell me what we can do inside those buildings that hasn't been done before. I want ideas, new approaches that I can push past Peary's objections. Above all, I want to find out what those machines are doing!''

One of the scientists muttered something to the man next to him. Lee ignored it.

"Let me remind you of what we've got to accomplish here. Sometimes when you're face-to-face with a problem every day, you lose perspective on it.

"Those machines were put here by an alien race. An enemy of mankind. The ruins on Mars were made by men and destroyed by aliens. The Martian script refers to a battle of some sort. Most anthropologists think the script is reciting folklore. I think it was a history book, or maybe a newscast.''

Charnovsky huffed loudly.

"The Neanderthals on Sirius were colonists. The aliens—the Others, they call them—blew up Sirius B, turned the star into a nova, to wipe out all the life on that colony. There's evidence that an intelligent settlement—either ours or theirs, the evidence is very scanty—existed on Van Maanen's Star. It too was destroyed by a nova explosion.

"For the past year, I've been cajoling the Earth's archaeologists and anthropologists to reexamine the fossile records of human prehistory. Even if the earlier human civilization that founded the Mars and Sirius colonies was completely destroyed by the Others, there ought to be some archaeological evidence somewhere. Most of my colleagues have battled these ideas with every ounce of their strength. A few have gone out and started digging. They've found, already, that some of our previous conceptions of the datings of various human fossils are badly in error. Naturally, they're placing most of their emphasis on the Neanderthal fossils, and fortunately there's plenty of fossil record available on the Neanderthals.

"It seemes perfectly clear to me that there was an earlier civilization on Earth, at least fifty thousand years ago, maybe much earlier. Perhaps it was a Neanderthal civilization, perhaps Sapiens. In either event, it met an alien race, the Others, who built those machines topside. We fought a war, and we lost. Our settlements on Sirius, on Van Maanen's Star, on Mars and the Moon were totally wiped out. The only known survivors are the Neanderthals on Sirius. The Others must have done an especially thorough job on Earth itself, to make certain that the planet would never foster an intelligent civilization again. But we survived. The Neanderthals didn't make it, but we did. Now we're able to reach the stars again. And the Others are probably out there somewhere, waiting for us."

Lee paused. No one moved.

Then Richards said, "That's a lot to swallow in one sitting."

"I know. And the details may be wrong. But I think the general picture is correct. Those machines up topside were built by the Others. Their purpose is hostile. They may still be out among the stars somewhere. If we expect to survive, we *must* understand what those machines are doing, and why. It's that simple."

Dr. Kulaki, a wiry electronics engineer, bobbed his head up and down. "Maybe the whole story's completely wrong, but who could take the chance of ignoring the possibility that it's right?"

"Exactly," Lee agreed. "That's why we're going to tackle those machines with every ounce of intelligence and strength in us. Neither Peary nor anyone else will stop us, that I guarantee you. Now I want your proposals for action by the end of the week."

Lee could feel the change in attitude throughout the underground community over the next few days. An invisible but almost palpable wave of tension swept through every office, every lab, every section of the tight-knit center. Not everyone believed Lee's theory about the Others, but they couldn't look at the alien buildings now without wondering.

Peary called him in to his office and said, "I hear you made quite a speech to the scientific staff a couple days ago. Got 'em all fired up."

"I told them what I thought we should be doing, and why."

The director scratched at his beard. "Good. Good. I want you to know that I'll back you all the way. Whatever you want, I'll do my best to help you get it." He cocked an eyebrow. "Provided, of course, you don't try tampering with the machines."

"I wouldn't dream of it," Lee said honestly. "Not until we understand them."

"See, they could be sending out a signal of some sort, and if we interrupt their functioning . . ."

"I know. I agree with you."

"Good. Long as we understand each other."

The next evening was Bennett's last on Titan, and the scientific staff threw a party for him. In his own quarters, since they were the largest available. The five-room apartment was jammed with people. Almost all of the hundred-odd scientists were there, plus many of the administrators and community workers. The party spilled out into the corridor. There was noise and laughter and the clatter of glasses and ice.

Lee and Marlene arrived at the same time, had a drink together, drifted apart, found themselves together again in a corner of Bennett's kitchen.

"Have you learned how to make coffee yet?" she asked, standing up close to him to be heard over the noise of the crowd.

He grinned. "Yes. It's not so tough, once you get the hang of it."

Somewhere music was playing and he wanted to dance with her, hold her, but there were too many people plastered too close together to do anything but talk and drink.

"Hello, Sid. You're blocking the icemaker."

He turned and saw Rich Lehman, blond, trim, tanned, and smiling.

"Oh. Hello," Lee said to the psychiatrist. He stepped away from the freezer. Lehman pushed his plastic tumbler into the ice slot and two big cubes chunked down into it.

"When did you get in?" Marlene asked Lehman.

"This morning, on the ship that's going to take Bennett out." He flashed his smile at both of them and then headed for the bar in the living room.

Lee watched him disappear into the crowd.

"What's the matter?" Marlene asked.

"He's here to keep an eye on me. It may not be the official reason for his coming to Titan, but he's following me."

Marlene did a double-take. "Sid, that's . . ." Her voice trailed off.

"I know. It's paranoid."

"Well . . ."

"You ask him and I'll bet he'll admit it. He started acting as my conscience back at Sirius. I think he enjoys the feeling of godhood it gives him."

With a slightly shaky laugh, Marlene said, "Who's analyzing whom?"

*   *   *

The last day of the week came. In the underground community each day looked exactly like every other day. But this morning, after Bennett's party, Lee awoke with a dull headache. *Charnovsky and his damned vodka.* After pills and coffee, he dressed and headed for the conference room.

He was the first one there and sat alone for a fidgety few minutes. Then the others filed in: Richards and Kulaki, talking earnestly together in the physics/electronics jargon that was half mathematical symbols; bearded Ray Kurtzman; somber-faced Petkovitch, the astronomer; Childe, mathematician; and Charnovsky, scowling with a hangover that he was too stubborn to admit to or medicate.

One by one, they went through their ideas and suggestions. Lee let them talk informally, didn't pick out the speaker, allowed them to hassle it out back and forth among themselves.

Gradually it became clear that the only one with a really new idea was Richards. Lee found himself wishing it had been someone else.

"There's a gravitational anomaly in the center of the building cluster," he explained. "Like the mascons on Luna, except smaller but more intense. If you compute the density of Titan and take a look at the stuff that this world's made of, you find pretty quick that the mascon at the buildings can't be natural. . . ."

"Very true," Charnovsky rumbled. "The densest material on this ice-puff is chondritic rock. No metals to speak of.''

"So there's a mascon at the site of the alien buildings," Petkovitch said, with a slight middle-European accent. "What does this prove?"

Richard turned his All-American smile on the astronomer. "Doesn't *prove* anything . . . yet. But why would they want such a concentration of high-density material? I think it's for power."

Kulaki burst in, "It could be the power source for the whole complex of buildings and machines. If it is, we might be able to trace the power flow and then learn who's doing what to whom!"

Lee sat back. "Do you really think so?"

Shrugging, Richards answered, "It's a place to start."

"Okay then. Let's get started on it."

"Wait a minute," said Kurtzman. He looked Lincolnesque in his beard, but his accent was from New York. "You're forgetting our friend Peary. To get at that mascon, we're going to have to rip out some of the machinery. . . ."

"Not if we tunnel in from the outside," Richards countered. "The mascon must go a long way below the surface. We can reach it by going under the buildings."

So he's thought that out too, Lee grumbled to himself, then felt even worse that he was displeased by Richards' thoroughness.

Kurtzman was saying, "I'll bet Peary still says no."

"Well, for what it's worth," Lee spoke up, "I don't intend to ask Peary for permission. I'm simply going to tell him what we're doing."

Kurtzman looked surprised, Richards pleased, the others halfway in-between.

"Start work on this now, this morning," Lee went on. "Gather the men and equipment you need. Alex, can you help them with the tunneling?"

Charnovsky nodded, wincing from his headache. "We must go through bedrock, of course. Drilling tunnels in the surface lawyers of ice is impossible unless you have elaborate equipment."

Lee said, "All right. Let's get moving on this. Now!"

They got up from their chairs, Charnovsky and Richards talking together, joined by Kulaki and Kurtzman. They looked and sounded eager. Petkovitch and Childe stayed on the fringes of the animated conversation.

Lee touched the phone button on the communicator panel set into the side of the table. "Mr. Peary, please." In less than a minute he made an appointment to see the director right after lunch.

Marlene was at the cafeteria. Lee told her about the meeting.

"And now you're going to tackle Peary," she said.

"Right."

She looked at him intently. "Sid, there's one other hurdle you've got to get over. The buildings themselves."

He said nothing.

"You've been here nearly a week without going out there. You're going to have to face it sooner or later."

Nodding, he asked, "Been talking to Lehman?"

She smiled at him but didn't answer.

"Okay. Right after my talk with Peary. I'll call you."

"Tunnel under the buildings?"

Behind his patriarchal beard, Peary looked startled. He edged forward in his contoured chair and put sweaty palms down on the desktop.

"That's right. We'll go through bedrock. Charnovsky will head the actual tunneling operation. We can easily avoid the building foundations."

"But why . . ."

"It's the mascon. Richards thinks it might be the power source for the machines, and the other scientsts feel he's probably right."

Peary blinked slowly. "But if you tamper with the power source you'll turn off the machines."

"We won't tamper with it. We just want to see what it is, where the power comes from, and where it's going."

"No," Peary said, shaking his head. "It's too risky. You might destroy something."

"Give those men credit for a little intelligence," Lee snapped. "They won't damage anything."

Peary's head kept swinging back and forth, his

eyes half shut. "No, I can't allow it. I can't . . ."

Lee's fists clenched. "We're doing it. This project has been agreed upon by the scientific staff. Unanimously. You can't stand in our way."

The director looked up and almost smiled. "You'll need to get your equipment requisitions signed. And your manpower allocations," he said slyly.

Lee could feel a hot flame trembling inside him. "If you get in our way, you'd better be prepared for a trip back to Earth to argue this out in front of the general chairman."

Peary's mouth dropped open. "Chairman O'Banion? Do you know him?"

"Not personally. But I'll take this fight straight to him, if you force me to. And I *do* know that he's spent his whole life trying to find out about these machines. His career's based on it—ever since he brought the first Jupiter mission back safely."

Peary fingered his beard again and shifted his gaze away from Lee. "Well now, there's no need to go all the way to O'Banion's level. No need to go Earthside at all. I'm only concerned with the problem of accidentaly harming the machines, and also about the safety of your men. Drilling tunnels . . ."

"Charnovsky knows what he's doing. We have enough laser equipment and conveyors to do the job, as long as we stay in bedrock."

"Well, I don't know. . . ."

"Come on, Charles. You'll be a hero, once we find the power source. It'll be the first major stride made here in years. O'Banion and everybody else Earthside will congratulate you."

"If it works."

"It will."

"And if there's no problems . . . or disasters."

You can always take the Japanese solution. Aloud, Lee answered, "Certainly there's some risk. But it's pretty small, I'm not going to let them run wild, I promise you that."

"Well . . . all right, I guess."

"Fine," Lee got up and left the director's office before Peary could change his mind.

Marlene was waiting for him in the dome topside, at the equipment lockers. She was already encased in a flame-red pressure suit. Lee found a suit that fit him and, with her help, wormed into it.

"I have a van ready for us at the main airlock," she said after they checked out each other's pressure seals and life systems.

With their bubble helmets under their arms, they clumped across the dome's plastisteel floor toward the parking area where several vans waited. Lee could feel his pulse starting to race. They entered the main airlock chamber, where a couple of technicians rechecked their suits and radios while another tech drove an electric van up for them.

Finally they climbed up into the van.

"Want me to drive?" Marlene asked.

"Okay," Lee slid over.

The air pumped out of the airlock chamber and the outer hatch slid open. Marlene turned on the van lights and they rolled out into Titan's unbreathable atmosphere.

There was no paved highway, but three generations of vans had worn a clearly discernible road into the ice surface. They crossed a bleak frozen plain, bluish-white in the dim twilight from the distant sun. The stars twinkling in the sky made the barren scene look even colder. The path climbed across a row of tumbled hills, and as they made a turn around the highest bluff, Saturn came into view.

"It's a compensation, isn't it?" Marlene said.

Lee nodded.

Saturn hung huge and low on the horizon, three times larger than Earth's full moon, casting shadows stronger than the sun's.

Soon they were down on the plain again, but now it was a shattered, broken expanse of jagged rock and ice, as if some huge fist had pounded it over and over again. A greenish methane cloud drifted over Saturn's circus-striped face, making the landscape even darker.

"There we are," Marlene said, looking straight ahead.

Lee saw the buildings and felt his throat go dry.

Marlene parked the van next to a pair of others,

near the wall of the nearest building. They loomed straight up from the dark, gloomy plain, gaunt specters with smooth polished walls. There were five squared-off featureless buildings ringed around a central pentagonally shaped tower that swept upward in a series of spires.

Lee made his hands stop shaking and put on his helmet. Then they popped the doors to the van and climbed down to the crunchy ice surface.

A single door had been cut into the wall in front of them. Lee remembered it from ages ago. He had been among the crew that had finally succeeded in pouring enough laser energy into the metallic wall to burn through it. No one else had dared to tamper with the buildings or the machines once they had gotten inside and seen what was there.

He could feel it sweeping over him as they walked the few steps from the van to the doorway: the tension, the twisting nerves, as if a deeply buried memory was writhing in his mind. Even before they stepped inside he could sense the driving, throbbing *purposefulness* of the machines.

And then they were inside, surrounded by them, row on row, tier on tier, inhuman, untiring, infallible machines humming, chattering, whining, filling the vast building with the rumbling power of their work. Driving, constantly driving at their unknown tasks. Along trackways that snaked through the maze of machinery, little oblong vehicles glided, levitated several centimeters off the track by some unknown force.

No matter where the two invading humans went along the twining trackways, one of these gray, snub-nosed vehicles hung behind them, vibrating like a tuning fork, *watching* them as if to make sure they didn't touch anything. The way a guard dog watches trespassing children.

He could feel it again—the alienness, the lurking presence of an intelligence that scorned the intruders from Earth. Every nerve in his body screamed the same message: get out, get away, this thing is evil, hostile, a weapon against all mankind. No matter what doubts anyone had about the reason for these machines, here Lee *knew*. This is the product of a cosmic hatred, the work of those who seek to destroy us, our ancient enemy, the unknown nameless Others.

"Are you all right?"

Marlene's voice in his earphones snapped him back to reality.

"Do I look green?"

She came up close enough so that their helmets nearly touched. "A little green," she said with a grin. "It gives me the creeps, too. Want to go?"

"Can we get to the mascon Richards is interested in?"

She looked at him. "Where the tower is?"

"I guess so."

"You really want to go in that deep?"

He nodded. "Yeah."

"All right."

They trudged slowly along the trackways, always followed by a guardian vehicle a few meters behind them. Lights had been strung by the human intruders long ago, and they reflected off Marlene's helmet, warped and distorted by its curve, as Lee followed her. Deeper into the maze of machines they went, while Lee's every nerve was screaming to get away. But he stayed behind Marlene, jaw clenched until it ached, making himself follow her, step by agonized step.

Down several levels they went, until finally Marlene pointed out across a catwalk railing to a shining metal cylinder as broad as a sequoia bole that sank down and down until it was lost in the darkness far below.

"That's it."

Lee leaned over the rail and peered into the shadows below. "I expected to see . . . something more mechanical."

"This is the center of the complex. The tower's straight over our heads."

Lee looked up, but rows of trackways and machinery tiers blocked his view. He had never been this deep inside the buildings before.

"Okay," he said. "Let's go back."

They walked in silence while the machines vibrated the ammoniated air around them. Then, at last, they were outside.

Lee found that he was sweating.

The other two vans were gone; theirs was the

only one parked on the rough icefield outside.
They climbed in, sealed the cab and lifted off their
helmets.

Lee let out a long, impassioned gasp of air.

"Sid, you did really well. I'm proud of you."

He tried to smile, but it was weak. "I feel like a
kid who's just dared the local bully and gotten
away with it."

"You deserve a drink."

He leaned back happily and let her drive the van
back to the dome.

Hours later, after several drinks and a dinner
that Marlene cooked herself, they were sitting together on the couch in her apartment, drinking
cognac and listening to music tapes.

"Where'd you get these snifters?" Lee asked her.

She swirled the brandy in the big graceful snifter.
"I always take them with me, wherever I go. I had
them on Sirius, we just never got a chance to use
them."

"You're kidding!"

"No. . . ."

He laughed and lifted his glass to her. "Ad
astra."

"Amen."

For a few moments the only sound in the room
was the music: dark, moody, restless.

"Answer me a question?" Marlene said.

"Sure, if I can."

"Why did your parents name you Sidney?"

He blinked. "Is this the beginning of a joke?"

"No, I'm curious."

"About my name?"

She nodded and suppressed a giggle.

"Well . . . my father was half Chinese and half
Spanish. My mother was an Irish Jew. I guess
Sidney was the only name they could agree on that
wouldn't offend the grandparents."

"It doesn't fit," Marlene insisted.

"I've never really cared for it."

"No . . . your name should be . . . ummm . . .
to go with Lee. Robert! No, that's been done.
Donald. Don Lee. No. Ralph? Samuel? Abraham!"

"You're drunk."

"Just a little. Do you like my music?"

"Very much. What is it?"

"Some early twentieth-century composer. Bach-
ianas Brasileiras. Number Eight, I think."

He leaned back on the couch and closed his eyes
listening. "Reminds me of topside, on the shore of
the ammonia sea. When the tide shifts."

Marlene nodded. "The wind, and the dark,
and . . ."

He turned his head to look at her; she was close
enough for him to smell the faint scent of her
cologne, to feel a wisp of her long auburn hair.

"You saved my life that day."

"Sid, don't . . ."

"Was it worth it? I've caused you a lot of grief,
haven't I?"

"No. Yes. . . . It's not your fault."

He slid his arm around her. She didn't resist it, but she didn't respond.

"It's taken me a long time to find out who I am and where I'm going," he said.

"Are you sure you know now?"

"Yes. I want to love you. I want you to love me."

"Sid, you only want me when you're alone, or hurt, or afraid."

"That's not the way it is anymore."

Softly, she leaned her cheek against his shoulder. Her voice was a whisper. "I loved you so much, and I never asked for anything except for you to love me. But you never did. I was born ninety-seven years ago. The doctors say that biologically I'm between thirty and thirty-five. I want babies, Sid. I want a daughter and a son."

For a long moment he could think of nothing to say. "I never . . . never thought about children."

Marlene straightened up to face him. "Love is a great and wonderful thing," she said dry-eyed, "and it heals all wounds and conquers all obstacles and turns ugly little girls into princesses. But I want babies. Two of them. Maybe more."

He heard himself chuckle nervously. "Right now?"

"We can start now, if you want to."

He ran out of words again.

Suddenly Marlene laughed. Not unkindly. "You should see your face. Oh my brave darling, you're so terrified. This is unfair to you . . . first the buildings and now this.''

"But . . .''

"No.'' She pulled away from his arms. "You'd better go. I'm sorry . . . I hate to make it sound so bitchy.''

Totally confused, he said, "Give me a chance to sort this out, Marlene. I . . .''

"Sid—Marty Richards asked me to marry him. He wants to take me away from all this and settle me down on some picturesque campus where we can ski in the winter and sail in the summer and make lots of babies.''

"Oh.''

"And I'm tired of being alone. I never realized how tired of it I was until Marty started filling my head with medieval romantic notions. Never realized how much mother instinct there is in me.''

"I see.'' All the old pain was suddenly flaming again, the memories of his own marriage, not the good part, not the earliest happy memories, but the hurt, the anger, the acid words.

Slowly he got up from the couch. "It . . . it's been one hell of a day,'' he said, trying to make it sound casual. It sounded fatal.

He got as far as the door, then turned and looked back at her. Marlene was still sitting on the couch, an indefinable smile on her lips.

"If it makes any difference to you,'' she said, "you're still the one I love.''

He held onto the door like a life raft.
"Thanks."

Weeks lapsed into months and the work on Titan inched along. Charnovsky led a team of tunnelers while Richards and Kulaki waited impatiently. Peary didn't actively hamper their work, but he didn't help speed it. Every requisition for equipment or material, every shift of personnel, every change in plans or needs was met by kilometers of red tape: forms to fill out, reports to dictate, mistakes to correct. Lee spent most of his time shuffling paperwork and computer tapes—and storming through the administrative staff. Peary himself smiled and nodded and agreed. It was like trying to run through quicksand.

But they forged on. Lee counted progress by the advance of the tunnel, meter by painful meter, through the bedrock under the ice. And the machines still ran with their mindless efficiency, doing whatever they were designed to do. Lee could hear the scornful laughter of the Others as the humans burrowed slowly toward the core of the machines. But now he also heard the laughter of humans. He didn't want to think of Marlene and Richards together, laughing at him. But he did.

He was sitting in the cafeteria, trying to forget about the paperwork that was heaped on his desk. It was late afternoon, the place was nearly deserted. Marlene was topside somewhere; most of the scientific staff were busy at tasks that were either necessary for the tunneling or busywork. The big wall screen was showing pictures of palm-decked tropical islands. It was supposed to be relaxing, Lee knew.

A quartet of men, led by Dr. Kurtzman, clumped in and punched coffee selections at the wall panel. They still had the lower halves of pressure suits on, and boots. Tiredly, they turned and headed for Lee's table.

They sat down, weariness etched on their faces. And something else—fear? Anger?

"Damned tunnel caved in on us," Kurtzman said. "We were lucky to get out alive."

"What? Was anybody hurt?"

Kurtzman nodded. "Two of Charnovsky's people. They were up front with the laser head. Pascual says they'll have to be shipped back to Earth."

Suddenly Lee felt as weary as they looked.

"I told them there was a pocket of ice up ahead," said one of the younger men, his face still grimy and set in a mask of anger and regret. "But they wouldn't listen to me; I'm not a geologist so they just didn't listen."

"How much of the tunnel went?" Lee asked.

Kurtzman shrugged. "Ten-fifteen meters. A day's work . . . double it, because now we'll have to go through it with extra bracing to make sure it doesn't fall in again."

"The laser head was smashed," said another of

the men. "We'll have to get a replacement."

"Which means a new requisition and a two-month wait."

"There's another head sitting in the communications center. It's a spare for them."

Shaking his head, Lee said, "Peary will never give permission to use the spare communications laser. He's going to be tough enough to settle down once he hears about the accident."

"We can 'borrow' the communications laser and modify it for tunneling. The guys there will let me take it. Peary and his people don't have to know that ours was smashed up."

Lee hiked his eyebrows, then grinned at them. "No comment."

"Why bother?" Kurtzman asked.

"Huh?"

Staring down at his coffee cup, Kurtzman said, "So we steal another laser and get lucky and finish the tunnel. So what? Do you really think we're going to learn anything about the machines?"

Lee stared at him.

One of the youngsters said, "But we've got to try, don't we? We'll never understand if we don't try."

"Bullcrap," Kurtzman said, slumping back tiredly in the plastic chair. "This isn't going to be solved by putting pieces together, like a puzzle. It's too big for us . . . those machines are beyond our mental capacity. Maybe in a century or two, or two hundred, we'll get smart enough to figure out what they're up to. But not now. They're so far beyond us that it's pathetic.''

The kid sputtered, "But that . . . that's unscientific!''

"So?" Kurtzman shot back. "Do you see science making any great strides around here? I'm a physical chemist; what the hell am I doing digging tunnels? We're in over our heads—no joke.''

One of the others, who had been silent until now, agreed. "We might as well quit. Forget it and go home. Let the machines go for another million years, if they want to. What difference does it make?''

"That would be fine, wouldn't it?" Lee said, his voice low and almost trembling with anger. "Give up and forget about it, without knowing where the machines came from, or what they're doing, or why.''

"How can we . . .''

"Listen to me. It's not just that they could be weapon against us. They might be, but that's not what's really important. Those machines mark the limit of our ability to understand the physical universe. Do you know what that means?''

Kurtzman sat up a little straighter in his chair.

"If we turn our backs on those machines,'' Lee went on, "we turn our backs on the basic premise of human thought. If we admit that we can't understand the machines then we admit that there's an absolute limit on our ability to understand the universe. We give in to the old witchdoctor's claim that there are some things in the world that man must not tamper with, Dr. Frankenstein. Taboo!''

"Yes, but . . .''

"The basic premise of scientific thought is at stake out there! We've got to understand the machines! Our claim to the stars, to survival on our own world, is tied up in it.''

Lee sat there on the edge of his chair, fists clenched, daring them to challenge his words. The young men stared back at him, looking surprised and perhaps even impressed.

Kurtzman broke the mood with a chuckle. "Okay, boss, we'll go back to the mines and dig some more. It's just a lucky thing for us that you never went into politics. You can be a helluva demagogue when you want to be.''

They completed the tunnel and celebrated. Then came the slow, hard work of examining the power core. Without interfering with it. An underground gallery was extended around the core's glistening super-metal cylinder. A shipful of new detection instruments soon clogged the gallery's rock floor.

Richards and Kulaki worked for months. They probed and measured and calculated and held long headache sessions that extended all night. The other scientists went about their routine work, helping when they could, but mostly powerless to assist.

Some scientists left, to be replaced by new men and women, faces young and eager to solve the riddle. Within weeks they aged noticeably.

Lee occasionally saw Marlene, but they both had walls built up between them now. They weren't strangers, but they behaved like strangers: polite, noncommittal, their lives touching only at the surface now.

Except once, when he accidentally met her in the surface dome as she was coming in from a four-day trek to observe a storm system that had built up over the tidal sea.

She was coming out of the locker area, tired and drained. Lee was on his way out to the tunnel, heading first for the lockers and a pressure suit.

They exchanged meaningless pleasantries for a moment.

"You've been working too hard," Lee said abruptly.

She shrugged. Looking upward toward the clear bubble of the dome. "It's good to see the stars again. After four days in the storm you begin to wonder if they're still there."

The dome was empty except for them. Lee stepped closer to her.

"That bright one there," she pointed, "is that Mars?"

"No, I think it's Jupiter."

"And where's Earth?"

He squinted and tried to ignore the distorted

light reflections in the plastic dome. "Can't find it. I think it's on the other side of the sun now."

Marlene said, "They look so lonely out there."

"Lehman would call that projection."

She turned toward him. "I know. We're the lonely ones, aren't we?"

He wanted to reach out, to hold her.

But she brushed her hair back wearily and said, "I've got to get some sleep. I'm just about wiped out."

"I'll walk you back to your place," he said.

"No. No, thanks . . . I wouldn't be much company for you." She tried a smile.

He didn't reply, just nodded and watched her walk slowly across the dome to the lift tube.

Richards and Kulaki were ready to make their report. The conference room was crowded, not only with the scientific department heads, but with as many of the scientists and administrators as could be squeezed in. Peary was there, sitting up at the head of the table, beside Lee. Marlene sat beside Richards.

When the room was absolutely filled, so that the last man in had to bring his own chair and plant it squarely in front of the door, Lee looked down the table to Richards.

"Okay, Marty, it's your show."

Richards stood up and walked toward the view-screen at the head of the room. Peary had to turn his chair around. The physicist looked confident, eager to tell what he'd found. He was grinning his feline grin again. Lee thought, *He'll have that boyish look to him even when he's eighty.* Marlene was watching him intently.

"Well, you all know that we've been poking into the power core down there in the salt mine," someone chuckled at that, "for the past four months. It's damned difficult to find out much about it in a passive way, but we've done the best we can." From the size of his grin, Lee judged that Richards was deliberately underplaying it.

He touched a dial set into the wall beside the viewscreen. The screen flickered into life, showing a hand-drawn graph.

"This shows what we've been able to learn about the power core. Which isn't a helluva lot. The key to it is the gravitational anomaly . . . it's a tremendous concentration of mass. We did a variation of Cavendish's experiment to determine the gravitational constant. . . ."

"Eighteenth-century physics," Kurtzman muttered.

"Yeah, but it works," countered Richards. "The material in that core has a density on the order of a thousand tons per cubic centimeter."

Petkovitch, the astronomer, looked skeptical. "But that's the density of degenerate material . . ."

"Like you find in white dwarf stars," Richards agreed. "Right."

The Pup's a white dwarf, Lee thought.

"But something that dense would sink right to the center of the planet," Petkovitch insisted.

Nodding, Richards said, "Sure. The cylinder must go down to the center. We've already started probe operations to check that out."

The audience stirred and began muttering.

Richards silenced them by raising his voice a notch until they quieted down. "Now, we haven't been able to determine just how they use this degenerate stuff to produce power . . . but my guess is that it's hydrogen inside there and they've got some sort of thermonuclear fusion reactor buried inside the cylinder. We detected strong magnetic fields, about nine hundred Tesla, up at the top of the cylinder. Very localized, though; like the field coils for a reactor would be."

Kulaki chimed in from his seat halfway down the table, in his brittle tenor voice, "You see, they probably are using the hydrogen in a degenerate state because you can pack more of it into a given volume that way. That's why the machines can run for millions of years!"

"If it's hydrogen," somebody remarked.

"It's hydrogen all right," Richards said. "I'm willing to bet on it."

No one offered serious disagreement.

"Now the next step is tougher," Richards said, looking straight at Peary. "We've got to put some sort of tracer on the energy coming out of the power core—where those strong magnetic fields are—and find out where the energy's going.''

"What kind of tracer?" Lee asked.

"There are electrical currents coming out of the top of that cylinder," Kulaki answered. "They ought to be very strong currents, but they're not—they're actually quite weak. We want to impose a modulating field on them, in pulses, so we can trace where the currents are going.''

Before Lee could admit that he didn't understand, Richards explained, "We can take one of the current paths and hit it with a short burst of energy that we create from our own equipment. Our burst will be a different frequency than the machine's current; it'll change the frequency of the machine's current by a very slight factor. But we can follow that slug of altered current as it goes through the machinery in the buildings, and find out where it's going.''

Suddenly Peary said, "That's tampering with the machines!"

"Only in the very slightest way. It shouldn't have any harmful effect on the machines.''

"You don't know that for sure!" Peary shouted, waggling a finger at the physicist.

"No," Richards admitted, "but all our calculations show . . .''

"Never mind. I have my orders. No tampering with the machines. I should never have taken the risk of letting you fool around with the power core. That's the end of it!'' He pulled himself out of his chair and turned toward Lee. ''This is your responsibility! No more tinkering with those machines *at all!* D'you understand? I don't want anybody out there, for any reason at all. And that's final!''

Peary stamped out of the room, pushing people aside in his haste to get to the door.

''He's gone crazy,'' somebody said.

Lee frowned at him.

Richards shrugged his shoulders. ''Well, boss, what do we do now?''

Lee could feel sheer fury welling up inside him. ''The meeting's over,'' he said, his voice low and flat. ''You can all leave. Except you, Marty.''

They all filed out, murmuring, shaking their heads. But Marlene stopped at the door and turned back.

''I want everybody out except Marty,'' Lee repeated.

''Let her stay,'' Richards said. He was grinning again; not quite as self-satisfied as before, but almost.

''All right,'' Lee said. He walked to the viewscreen and turned off the slide that was still being shown. Turning back to them, he said:

''Where in the hell do you keep your brains? Are you so goddamned smug that you really didn't know how Peary would pop his cork? I told all of you that Peary is my problem, that I'll handle him. Now you've pushed him into shutting down everything. All the work we've done and all we want to do—down the tubes, because you had to have a moment of glory.''

Richards' grin dropped into open-mouthed shock. ''Hey, look, I didn't mean to——''

''Stuff it. Now I'm going to have to move heaven and earth just to keep this work alive.''

''Honest, Sid, if I . . .''

Lee glanced at Marlene, then back to Richards. ''Listen. If I have to ship you out of here to placate that ass, that's just what I'm going to do.''

''Now wait a minute . . .'' Richards was starting to get red-faced.

''I just want to let you know where it stands,'' Lee said. ''You've screwed up royally. Now I've got to make good on a threat I've been holding over Peary . . . and I don't know if it'll work.''

''What do you mean?'' Marlene asked.

''I've got to call Earthside, the general chairman.''

''O'Banion?'' Richards asked.

''Right.''

Lee didn't notice Marlene's little gasp of surprise, nor the sudden look of fear that flickered in her eyes.

The general chairman sat dozing in his contour chair. His private office was small and bare, utilitarian; a vast contrast to the sumptuous office that the public saw, ornate with the trappings of power. And responsibility.

The communicator on his desk chimed softly. He opened his eyes. "Yes, what is it?"

"Sir," a woman's voice replied, "there's a call from the Titan station requesting your personal attention. From a Dr. Sidney Lee."

Lee? Lee. The name was somehow familiar. The general chairman frowned with concentration as he tried to remember. At moments like these, he looked his hundred-plus years, despite all the plastics and hormones of the meditechs. His hair was dead white, his face lined, eyes vague and sometimes drifting. And on his throat were two jagged scars, now nearly hidden by wrinkles, that he had refused to have removed when his artificials gills had been taken out.

"Lee," he muttered. He touched a button on his desk and the viewscreen on the far wall began to glow.

"Dr. Sidney Lee," the general chairman said to the computer behind the screen. "Full personnel file."

Almost immediately the screen showed Lee's picture and history: birth, education, marriage, divorce, assignment to Titan, mental breakdown, recovery, the Sirius mission, reassignment to Titan. A whole life in a half-dozen succinct lines.

"There is a personal comment on the file, sir," the computer said, in a warm feminine voice.

"Let's hear it."

"Lee, Sidney: cross-reference Ettinger, Marlene."

The general chairman nodded. "Yes, I know. I remember."

The viewscreen faded.

He turned to the communicator again. "Tell Dr. Lee that I can't be disturbed. Have Majeski take his call; tell him to be polite but noncommittal. Then tell Majeski to see me."

"Yes, sir."

He flicked the communicator off. *They're together on Titan now. The two of them. Still young. The two of them.*

Suddenly he was laughing, a wheezing private cackle, laughing to himself and thinking, *What would Osawa and the rest of the opposition think if they knew why I've battled so hard to stay in power for so long? What would they think?*

Then he found himself staring at the computer viewscreen. For a moment he thought of asking for the file on Marlene. But he didn't need it. Even with the screen blank he could see her face as clearly as ever.

Weeks passed. Without word from the general chairman, without authority to trace the circuitry of the machines, the scientists on Titan went back to meaningless humdrum. Peary bustled about and noisily let everyone know that he was arranging a series of tours from Earth, so that everyone from schoolchildren to religious pontiffs could see the works of the Others.

Lee stared at the bleak towers and the bleaker men, trying to use the little knowledge they had to theorize the meaning of the machines. *The blind men and the elephant*, he thought.

He was having coffee in the cafeteria one afternoon when Richards came up and sat across the table from him.

The .physicist was wearing his see-what-I've-done grin once again.

"Still sore at me?" he asked boyishly.

Lee tried to smile back but he knew it didn't come out well. "No, I guess not," he lied.

"Look, Kulaki's on to something. It might turn out to be a dead end, but . . . well, listen. When we were making the gravitational measurements at the power core, there were occasional fluctuations in the measurement. Just tiny flicks. We thought they were random flukes in the instruments, so we didn't bother mentioning them. But the more I thought about it, the more it bothered me. Sure, there's always noise in a measurement . . . but there are reasons for it."

Lee made a noncommittal sound.

"So we reran all the data tapes on the measurements we made down there, and sure enough, those fluctuations happen 'way too often to be instrumental noise. No particular pattern to them, but they show up too much to be accidental."

"What does it mean?" Lee asked.

Richards hunched forward, propping his elbows

on the table. "Kulkai thinks the machines are broadcasting gravity waves."

"Gravity waves?"

"Yep. I know it sounds a little weird, but it might explain why nobody's ever been able to find any signal being beamed from the buildings, even though the towers sure look like an antenna system of some kind. We've always looked for electromagnetic radiation. But if the tower's broadcasting gravity waves . . . ."

"But why? What's the purpose?"

The physicist shrugged. "One thing at a time. We just might have a line on what all that machinery is doing."

Nodding, Lee admitted, "You just might, at that."

"Okay then," Richards said, "you're the boss. What do you want to do about this idea?"

"Check it out, obviously. How the hell do you measure gravity waves, anyway?"

"It can be done. But if we're going to make any sense out of this, we ought to check it out in space—see where the radiation is being sent and how far into space it goes."

"Can you do that?"

Richards shrugged. "It'll be a bitch of a job. The measurements have to be damned sensitive and precise. And it'll be expensive."

With a sardonic grin, Lee said, "I get the point. I'll have to tackle Peary again. . . . Well, at least we won't be touching his precious machines. Maybe he'll be glad to get a few of us off-planet.''

Richards winced, and Lee realized what a projection he had just made.

After ten days of discussing, debating, and occasionally violent shouting matches, the scientific staff agreed on a plan for measuring the gravitational waves being beamed by the machines. Lee took a three-page digest of the plan to Peary. The final page had the cost numbers on it.

Peary looked aghast at the cost.

''That's more than our annual budget!''

''I know,'' Lee said. ''It's about what this first round of tourist visits is going to cost.''

''Too expensive. Earthside will never approve it. I wouldn't even have the nerve to ask them.''

''But it's the most important stride forward in our understanding that we've ever made.''

''If it works.''

''It will.''

Peary scratched at his beard. ''There's nothing I can do about it.''

''You can ask the Council to let us use the money they've already allocated for the tourists . . .''

''What? Never! That's all set up, I'm not going to ruin all my plans.''

''And I'm not going to let you spend that money on nonsense when there's useful work to be done!'' Lee snapped.

"Oh no?" Peary chuckled. "Then why don't you put in another call to your good friend the general chairman? Maybe he'll answer your first call at the same time."

Lee got up and stormed out of the director's office.

It was late that same night. Lee was sitting up on his bed, too tense to sleep, too tired to work. His mind kept churning thoughts, faces, voices, over and again, useless fragments of memories parading in random order.

The door chime sounded. Frowning, Lee pulled on a zipsuit as the chime went off again. He padded barefoot to the door and opened it.

Marlene.

"I heard about your talk with Peary," she said, without preliminaries.

He ushered her into the living room, shut the door behind her.

She stood before him, tall and lovely and very grave. "Sid, O'Banion won't answer you. He won't see you or talk to you."

Her voice was so strong, so certain.

"What do you mean?" he asked.

"Robert O'Banion, the general chairman . . . the one who was on the first Jupiter mission. He's not going to answer your call. Not ever."

Lee stared at her. Then, stepping slowly away from the door, he said, "I think we'd better sit down."

So they sat together on the couch and she told him about Bob O'Banion. She spoke softly, calmly, hardly a hint of emotion in her voice. But her eyes showed it, her deep brown eyes and her hands, clenching as she spoke.

And when she was finished, all he could say was, "My God, I've screwed up your whole life, haven't I?"

For an answer she threw her arms around his neck and they were together again. At least for a little while.

The general chairman was at home when her call came through. It was early morning. He usually rose early, had a breakfast of juice and concentrates, and then went through as much of the day's paperwork as possible before his ceremonial duties captured him. *I still work harder at a hundred and fifteen than Osawa does at sixty.*

He was at breakfast when the viewscreen at his elbow chimed. He turned to it, and the secretary told him who was calling. He had expected it, but it still took him so much by surprise that he sucked in his breath for a moment and could not speak. Clearing his throat, he said:

"All right. Put her on."

He turned the communicator off. It would be an hour and twenty-some minutes before his decision to talk to her could reach Titan, even at the speed of light. And an equal time before her face and voice could come to him.

O'Banion touched the communicator switch again and said to the secretary, "Cancel everything for today. I'm not feeling well."

"I'll send Dr. Mor——"

"No. Just cancel and express my apologies."

The secretary still looked concerned. "Yes, sir. I'll cancel all engagements and calls."

"Except the one from Titan. I'll take that one here when it comes in."

"Yes, sir."

He was in the garden when the call came through. The general chairman was constrained to live near Messina, where the world government had built its capital. But O'Banion's garden was a desert blossoming, not the semitropical lushness of the Mediterranean. He had cactus and moonflowers set into bare dry soil; no ponds or sprinklers or hint of water. Certainly no aquatic life of any kind anywhere near him. A high wall with an acoustic barrier kept the nearby sea out of sight and sound.

The communicator chimed from the house, so he walked back through the garden slowly, with the careful steps of an old man. He settled himself in a contour chair next to the open garden doors, with the warm Sicilian sunlight baking him. *Like a lizard*, he always thought.

Her face took form on the viewscreen as he sat down. She had hardly changed at all from his last memory of her: auburn hair still long and flowing, those soul-deep eyes, stubborn chin and finely chiseled bone structure, skin meant for caressing.

And that maddening serious expression on her face, as if there could be something in this world more important than loving her.

"Bob, the secretary who set up this call said we'd be talking in private. I wondered when Sid first tried to reach you if you'd remember me at all. The fact that you haven't answered him, yet you're listening to me, means that you do remember after all."

You know damned well I could never forget you.

"If it makes any difference to you, I'm still in the same boat I was in the last time we saw each other. I love him, Bob. I wish I didn't, but I do. And he loves me, I know he does, but he's possessed by those machines. They've become an obsession with him—he's using them to keep a protective wall around himself, focusing all his feelings on the machines so that he won't have to risk getting hurt by people again. I've hurt him, and so have other people. So he uses the machines to keep from getting hurt again. It's . . . No, that's not why I'm calling."

She pushed a wisp of hair back from her face. "Bob, I really don't know much about you now, or how you feel about everything, except that you refused to take Sid's call and you've accepted mine. I hope that doesn't mean you're angry at him . . . or at me. We need your help. Not just Sid, or me, but everybody here on Titan. The whole human race, really. You're the only one who can help us. We've got to learn to understand those machines. You know that. You've given your whole life to it.''

That's what everyone believes. How noble of me.

''But, if you turn him down, you'll be killing him. He's fought so hard, he's been holding onto himself for so long, if you defeat him it'll be the end of him. It will destroy him, and me too.''

What is that to me?

''Please listen to him, Bob. He needs your help. We all need your help. I think perhaps we can find out what the machines are doing, and why . . . but you're the only man who can let us accomplish it. If you don't help us, then the Others win, and we lose. You, Sid, me . . . all of us.''

Abruptly the picture shut off.

The secretary came on the screen immediately. ''The transmission seems to have been cut off from Titan, sir.''

''Yes, it's all right.'' *She didn't want me to see her crying.*

He sat there in the sun, an ancient man still simmering with the memories of youth, feeling robbed, feeling angry, feeling . . . what? *Love? At your age?* He almost laughed at himself.

The secretary was still on the screen. ''Sir, will there be an answer? Should I try to get them back?''

"No," he said. Then, "Wait, I have an answer. Private line, for Dr. Ettinger only. Personal and confidential."

"Yes, sir." The secretary's face vanished and the screen went pearl-white.

"Marlene: I've spent the better part of a century waiting for this moment. I've loved you and hated you at the same time for all these years. I suppose, in a way, you've been responsible for my career in political power. In my most private dreams, I've longed for the day when you knelt at my feet. Now it's come. And I'm starting to feel like some foolish character playing the role of an evil nobleman in an Italian grand opera.

"There's no enjoyment in a revenge that waits so long. Still, there's a part of me that wants to take that revenge. So we'll strike a compromise; a bargain. I'll give Lee what he wants as far as those buildings are concerned. But you must leave Titan and return to Earth. I want you here, in Messina, close to me. I'll find a position on the scientific staff here for you. I want to see you in the flesh. And I want you to see me.

"In case you're wondering, the doctors tell me that sexual stimulation is bad for my heart. Even plastic hearts have limits to them. But there are clinical techniques for initiating pregnancy. If you're willing to live up to that side of the bargain, I'll approve Lee's plans."

Hating himself, he touched the Off switch of the communicator.

Marlene didn't tell Lee about the bargain, only that O'Banion would talk to him.

Within a week, the plan was approved. Richards and Kulaki started requisitioning the equipment they'd need. Half the scientific staff on Titan began to help him, and fresh recruits began arriving from Earth. Peary scowled and cowered and watched his tourist deal evaporate before his eyes.

Before a second week was out, Richards ran a jury–rigged experiment out on the ice fields near the edge of the tidal sea and came back triumphantly. His equipment had detected gravitational waves, sharply focused in a narrow beam, coming from the direction of the tower.

"The machines *are* broadcasting gravitational energy," Richards said, smiling hugely with success. "They're beaming it inward through the solar system. Toward Earth!"

"But why?" asked Lee.

That's when the reaction started to set in. So they knew what the machines were doing. But what was the reason for it? There as no discernible effect on Earth. Dropping a penny off a skyscraper roof released more energy than the gravitational pulses from the machines seemed to be emitting.

We're like children, Lee thought, *trying to put together a stereo transceiver from an assembly kit.*

All the pieces are here, but we don't know how to get them together in the proper way.

He officiated through a desultory meeting of the scientific staff, where Richards' well-known results were officially reported and plans for the spacecraft measurements at various points between Saturn and Earth were discussed.

At the end of the meeting, Lee stood up at his place at the head of the table and said with an enthusiasm he really didn't feel:

"Considering where we were just a few months ago—and for many, many years before that—I think Marty and Gene Kulaki have made an enormous contribution. I've recommended them for the World Science Award."

The scientists around the table really applauded that. Kulaki looked surprised and slightly embarrassed. Richards looked pleased and nodded an acknowledgment of their applause.

And Lee smiled to himself. *You'll be spending a year or more inside a spacecraft lab, friend. Hope you enjoy your fame.*

As he was leaving the conference room, Donald Childe, the short, waspish mathematician, approached him.

"I've been talking over an idea with Petkovitch," he said. "It might be nothing more than a mathematical exercise, but on the other hand . . ."

"What is it?" Lee asked. They were out in the

corridor now, walking slowly toward the living quarters area.

"Well, we found out about the power core because of its gravitational anomaly: the mascon effect," Childe said in his flat New England twang. "We found the mascon effect because it perturbed the orbits of the communications satellites we've got going around Titan. Those orbits have been tracked continuously for damn near a century. They ought to show another perturbation—an infinitesimal one, maybe—for every time the machines send out a pulse of energy. If we can plot those perturbations, we can see what kind of pattern the machines have been working on for the past century."

"Hmm."

"Wouldn't cost much," Childe said, like a Yankee. "Just some pencils and paper and computer time."

"Can you really trace the perturbations if they're so small?"

"Don't know," the mathematician answered with a shrug. "But if we can, we might be able to find out if there's some pattern to the machines' operation."

"I guess it's worth trying," Lee said.

Childe grinned at him. "Good."

When Lee got back to his quarters, Marlene was there.

"Hello," he said as he shut the door. Surprises always left him tongue-tied.

She was sitting on the couch, coiled up, tense.

"I wanted to talk to you, Sid. I . . . I've been putting it off, but . . ."

"What's the matter?" He sat down beside her.

Her fists were clenched in her lap. "I want to leave Titan. I've got to. As soon as possible."

"Leave? Why—" Then it hit him. "Oh, I get it. You want to go with Richards."

She almost smiled. "No, it's not that simple. I'm going back to Earth."

"Earth?"

"Yes. And right away, the sooner the better."

Shaking his head in puzzlement, Lee asked, "Marlene, what's this all about? Why are you so uptight?"

"I've . . . been offered a position on the scientific staff at the world government headquarters. In Messina."

Lee couldn't fathom the strange expression on her face: there was absolute fear in her eyes, and something more. She was searching for something.

"Wait a minute, let me get this straight," he said. "You want to leave and take a position in Messina."

She nodded wordlessly.

"Why?"

"What difference does that make?" she snapped. "My work here is finished. There's very little more I can do in the way of atmospheric physics research."

"That's not true and you know it."

She didn't answer.

"It's because Richards is leaving and you don't want to be stuck here with me, isn't it?"

"Sid, you're such an idiot."

His temper was rising. "Well then, what the hell is it?"

"Would it make any difference to you what it is?" she asked quietly. "I'm going to Earth and there's nothing you can do to stop me."

"I can refuse to sign your transfer request."

She shrugged. "Then I'll resign and ship out as a private citizen."

"I just don't understand it. . . ."

"That's right, you don't."

"And you're not going to tell me why you're leaving."

"I'm leaving; that's the only part of it that you need to know."

He slammed a fist on the arm of the couch and got to his feet. Looking down at her, he said, "All right, then. Go! Fill out a transfer form and I'll sign it."

She rose to face him. Her voice shaky for the first time, she answered, "I'll have the transfer request on your desk tomorrow morning."

The yellow coded card was on his desk when he got to his office the next morning, coolly typed out and signed in the proper place.

Lee sat at the desk and stared at it for a long time. He pictured himself tearing it to shreds, but knew that she would merely make out another. *Face it,* he told himself. *It's been over for a long time.*

The phone buzzed and he saw her face on the screen before his hand could flick the switch. But it was Lehman instead.

"Oh. What is it?"

"Nothing important," the psychiatrist said cheerfully. "Your annual examination is due, and I thought I'd remind you about it."

Lee could feel his face tensing into a frown. "Do you call every staff member with a personal invitation?"

"No, not usually." Lehman's face went serious. "I . . . uh, I saw Marlene last night. She was pretty upset. She wouldn't say what it was about, just that she leaving."

"So you want to get me into your dream machine and see if I'm about to flip my libido again."

With a sudden laugh, Lehman said, "You still have these quaint notions about us psyche-patchers, don't you?"

"Listen, Rich, stop trying to be my conscience. Or whatever it is that you're trying to do. I don't know how you get your kicks, but they're not going to be at my expense."

Lehman pursed his lips in an inaudible whistle. "My, you're touchy this morning. I'm only trying to help you, friend."

"When I want your help I'll ask for it." Lee snapped off the connection.

He looked back at Marlene's transfer application, then reached for his stylus and angrily signed it.

For a week Lee fumed in helpless frustration. Marlene's transfer request was automatically approved and she would leave on the next ship. It was due at the end of the week.

The scientific work on Titan had settled back largely into routine. Richards and Kulaki were waiting for their ships and equipment. But Childe and a few computer techs were as busy as politicians a week before election day. The little mathematician was literally burying himself under rooms full of data tapes that went back more than ninety years.

The day that Marlene's ship landed, Childe burst into Lee's office.

"I've got it! It's all here!"

Lee jumped out of his chair. "What? What is it?"

The mathematician was almost too excited to speak. "The data . . . it's all here . . . ninety-four years worth of satellite perturbations . . . look at them, aren't they beautiful?"

He unrolled a long spool of paper tape that was covered with multicolored wiggling lines. Lee blinked at them.

"There's the pattern of pulses that the machines have been putting out for the past ninety-four years!'' Childe's grin was face-splitting. ''It's all there, just like I said it would be.''

Nodding in bewilderment, Lee said, ''Okay, fine . . . but what does it mean?''

Pointing to the long roll of paper unfurled across his office floor, Lee asked, ''What significance is there to the pattern? What does it tell us?''

Childe frowned. ''How would I know? I'm a mathematician, not an engineer. I found the pattern, now it's up to somebody else to figure out what it's good for.''

Lee closed his eyes. ''Thanks.''

He spent that night alone in his apartment, drinking quietly, steadily, until he fell into a dreamless sleep. In the morning—the morning that she was leaving—he awoke in his chair feeling stiff all over, and with a thundering headache. He staggered painfully into the bathroom.

Showered and medicated, he came out feeling better. Until he saw the clock. *My God, she's taking off right now!*

He raced through the corridors and up the lift tube, bolting out onto the dome's broad floor just in time to see the shuttle rising up into the dark sky on a sheath of plasma flame. A muted roar shook the dome slightly. There were a dozen or so people standing around, watching the takeoff.

He stood there burning, burning, every cell of his body feeling the hot flame of the rockets.

Abruptly he spun about and ducked back into the lift tube. Down to his office he went, slammed himself down in his desk chair and punched the phone switch.

"Communications center," he snapped.

"Communications here."

"This is Dr. Lee. That shuttle that just took off, recall it."

"What?" The communications tech's face looked startled.

"Recall it. Top priority. Now!"

"But Dr. Lee, it's due to rendezvous with the main ship . . . and the schedules . . ."

"Fuck the schedules! Call her back!"

White-faced, the tech nodded, "Yes, sir."

"And get me a direct line to Dr. Ettinger, on board that shuttle."

"Yes, sir. It'll take a few minutes. . . ."

"Stop talking about it and do it."

The screen went blank momentarily, but almost at once Lee's secretary's face appeared on it. "Dr. Lee, Dr. Petkovitch has been trying to reach you . . . he called earlier, before you arrived at the office. Shall I call him back?"

"Later."

"He seemed very insistent."

"Later!"

The communications tech came back on the screen. "I have Dr. Ettinger, sir. The transmission is a little weak because of the plasma interference."

Lee silenced his excuses with a wave of his hand.

Marlene's face appeared on the screen. She looked surprised, almost worried.

"Sid, what's this all about? They said you've ordered the shuttle back. . . ."

"That's right. Either you stay on Titan or I go with you to Earth. There's no third way."

Her eyes widened. "Wh . . . what did you say?"

"You heard it. Which do you prefer?"

"You can't leave Titan."

"Want to bet?"

"But . . . Sid, I must go back to Earth. I can't stay."

"Then I'm going with you."

"No, you can't. You don't understand. . . ."

"You can explain it to me on the way to Earth."

"It's impossible."

He made a cutting motion with his hand, a gesture he had unconsciously picked up from Ardaka. "Everything's impossible until you try. I love you, Marlene. It's taken me all my life to say it, all my life to realize that I mustn't lose you. I don't care what it costs or how much pain there is with it. I love you, and if we're not going to be together, it won't be because I didn't try."

Laughing in spite of herself, she said, "You're crazy!"

"That's right. But this is the good kind."

"Oh, Sid, if only . . ."

"It'll work, don't worry. We'll make it work."

"You'd really leave Titan?" she asked warily.

"Why do you think I've called the shuttle back?"

"After all this has meant to you? You can just walk away from it?"

He reached both hands out toward the screen, toward her serious, doubting, beautiful face. "Marlene, you mean more to me than anything else. That's what I've learned. I want to spend what's left of my life with you."

And suddenly she was smiling and crying at the same time. "It's not fair . . . the things you can do to my equilibrium . . ."

Grinning, he replied, "I'll see you when you land."

She nodded and cut the connection.

Immediately the phone chimed again and Lee's secretary came on the screen. "Dr. Petkovitch is here; he wants to see you most urgently."

With a shrug, Lee answered, "Okay, okay. Send him in."

The office door opened and the dark-bearded astronomer shuffled in. His eyes were sunken and bloodshot, but there was a whacked-out grin on his face. *He's high,* Lee thought. *But on what?*

"Sit down," Lee said. "You look punched out."

Petkovitch slumped into the chair before Lee's desk. He almost giggled. "Been up thirty . . . no forty-two hours straight. No sleep. Working with Childe."

"On the . . ."

"The patterns," the astronomer finished for him. "They fit. They actually fit. It's . . ." He shook his head, completely run out of words.

Lee blinked at him. "They fit *what?*"

"The sunspot cycles." Petkovitch laughed, almost like the beginnings of a hysterical fit. "The sunspot cycles . . . what else? What else could it have possibly been. Ali this time, and it was staring us in the face!"

Lee could feel himself sinking back into his chair. His voice sounded hollow. "You're certain?"

Suddenly irritated, the astronomer snapped, "No, of course we're not certain! We just worked it out roughly. But the correlation looks good. We need the Central Computer Network at Great Lakes to confirm it fully."

"The machines are causing sunspots?"

Petkovitch nodded. "Sunspots, and their associated solar flares and most of the other types of disturbances of the photosphere. No wonder we've never been able to predict solar flares with a single theory. We never realized . . ."

But Lee had stopped listening. Suddenly it was blindingly clear to him. He saw Sirius' Pup exploding. He saw the same forces unleashed by the Others on the sun . . . mankind's sun . . . torturing it into an agonized series of upheavals that sprayed radiation throughout the solar system.

"They destroyed the Neanderthals by making the Pup go nova. And the sun . . ."

Petkovitch said, "The sun's not massive enough for that type of nova. But these machines can cause sunspots, flares, constant agitation. You know, every ten thousand years or so there's a truly major flare, the kind that caused the Libian Glass—thousands of square kilometers of desert sand fused into glass . . ."

"The radiation from flares like that could be lethal on Earth's surface."

Nodding, Petkovitch said, "Unless we evolved resistance to such radiation levels."

"The machines were set up to cause the flares, to kill us off, to keep Earth sterilized."

His eyes closing with weariness, Petkovitch agreed, "It looks that way."

"Then the machines failed!"

The astronomer's eyes snapped open.

"They failed." The knowledge warmed Lee like sunshine melting frost. "The Others failed . . . their goddamned machines haven't killed us."

"But we still don't know how they work."

"We'll find out how," Lee said. "We can go in there now and dismantle them and see what makes them tick. Think of what's in there for us to learn! A technology that's centuries ahead of us!"

"And it was built millennia ago. What are the Others doing now?"

Lee shook his head. "No matter. They're not gods or devils. We can understand what their machines are doing; they're not beyond the scope of human intelligence. *That's* the most important discovery of all.''

Petkovitch sat up a little straighter. ''I had forgotten that aspect of it . . .''

But Lee was musing, ''Where do the Neanderthals fit in? Did our two species coexist on Earth? And just who are the Others? Where did they come from? Are they still alive out there, someplace?''

''Good Lord, the more questions we answer, the more unanswered questions there are.''

The phone chimed and Lee punched at its keyboard.

''The shuttle will be landing in fifteen minutes, Dr. Lee.''

''Thanks.''

Turning to Petkovitch, he said, ''Get some sleep. When you wake up, you'll be head man around here. I'm heading back for Earth on that shuttle.''

Startled, the astronomer sputtered, ''Wh . . . what . . . you can't just . . . there's too much . . .''

Lee grinned at him. ''It's all yours, friend. I've walked my bloody mile. I'm finished with it.''

''But this sunspot theory might be completely wrong! And there's still . . .''

''You can handle it. And even if your theory is wrong, at least we're cutting the machines down to human size. Nobody's going to worship them. Not when we can understand them. Maybe not today . . . but soon.''

"You can't just . . . leave everything."

"The hell I can't." In his mind's eye he could see Marlene, and the troubled look haunting her eyes. There was something she hadn't told him yet, something deep and aching. *But it doesn't matter*, he thought. *We can make it if we face it together*.

With an almost boyish grin he got up from the desk and came around it to clasp Petkovitch's shoulder. "It's all yours. You'll have the honor of officially solving the mystery. You'll get into all the history books. Good luck."

"But . . ." the astronomer still seemed dazed. "But you . . . what about you?"

"Me?" Lee laughed. "I'm going to catch the shuttle. I'm going home."

AFTERWORD: THE SAGA OF "THE OTHERS"

Ah, love, let us be true
To one another! for the world, which seems
To lie before us like a land of dreams,
So various, so beautiful, so new,
Hath really neither joy, nor love, nor light,
Nor certitude, not peace, nor help for pain;
And we are here as on a darkling plain,
Swept with confused alarms of struggle and flight;
Where ignorant armies clash by night.
—Matthew Arnold, *Dover Beach*

What better image to inspire a science fiction story? What better description of the creative act of scientific research itself, where armies of dedicated men and women have for centuries toiled willingly to shrink their ignorance and shed some light on the "darkling plain" of our existence.

Yet the novel *As On a Darkling Plain* originated not with Arnold's haunting poem, but with the pair of quotations given at the start of the book:

The Universe is not only queerer then we imagine—it is queerer than we *can* imagine.
　　　　　　　　　　　　—J.B.S. Haldane

Clarke's Third Law: Any sufficiently advanced technology is indistinguishable from magic.
　　　　　　　　　　　　—Arthur C. Clarke

It was not until the novel was almost finished that I chose the line from Arnold's *Dover Beach* for its title.

As On a Darkling Plain is, of course, part of a series of interlinked novels that may be loosely described as the saga of "The Others." The first of these novels was *The Star Conquerors*; the last of them (or perhaps I should say merely the latest) is *Orion*. Unlike many science-fiction series, in which a "future history" of the human race is plotted out beforehand and stories written to fill in the blank places in the outline, the saga of The Others grew organically. I had no intention, originally, to write a series of stories. In fact, I had no intention to write such stories at all.

What happened was this:

In 1949, when I was working on a Smith-Corona portable atop an orange crate (literally!) in the cellar of my parents' home in South Philadelphia,

I decided to write a science fiction novel about—what else?—the first journey to the Moon. The hero of this novel was an American astronaut named Chester A. Kinsman. The basic plot of the story was that the Russians started a space program before the Americans did, and were well on their way to establishing a manned space station in orbit around the Earth as a steppingstone on their way to the Moon. In 1949 every science fiction enthusiast knew that "whichever nation controls the Moon controls the Earth." So the United States mounted a crash program to get Americans on the Moon before the Russians could get there.

It all sounds rather quaint now. But by the time I finished the novel, in the early 1950s, the basic idea apparently startled the editors to whom I hopefully sent the manuscript. It was rejected, time and again, a process that literally took years because each publishing house held onto the manuscript for many months before sending it back to me.

You can imagine how dog-eared it became. I seem to recall that a few editors were kind enough to enclose short personal notes of the "try again" variety, although most times the battered box of pages came back with nothing more than a printed rejection form.

In truth, it was a poorly written novel, as most first novels are. Its main usefulness turned out to be that in the writing of it, I learned a good deal about how to write fiction. Nothing teaches like doing.

When I had finally exhausted all the New York publishing houses I could think of, I sent the manuscript to a local Philadelphia publisher, the Winston Company, which in those days was putting out a line of science fiction novels for teenagers. Lester Del Rey, one of my idols, was among the contributors to this line. In those days of the 1950s, "juvenile" novels were a very important part of the hardcover book market for science fiction writers. Robert A. Heinlein was writing juveniles for Scribner's; Isaac Asimov was doing the same under his Paul French *nom de plume* for Doubleday.

I was fortunate enough to hit an editor who cared enough about his work to send me an encouraging letter. Donald E. Cooke even invited me to his office in midtown Philadelphia for a face-to-face discussion of my novel. Brimming with wonder and with hope, I rode the trolley car up to the building where the Winston Co. was headquartered. Cooke was very gracious. He said, essentially, that even though he was not going to buy my novel, he wanted me to write something else for him.

He explained that my writing was not as bad as some work he had seen in print. But the plot for my novel, the idea that the Russians would get into space ahead of the United States, stirred some misgivings. There was a Senator Joseph McCarthy

(R., Wisc.) raging through the land in those days of the 1950s, finding Communist subversion wherever he looked. Cooke told me that if Winston published a novel hinting that the Soviets were smarter than we were, even in something as arcane as space exploration, McCarthy would make his life and mine unbearable.

He advised me to go home and try writing something else, something that had no connection whatever with current or near-future politics.

I was both elated and crushed. On the one hand, my novel had been rejected again. (Its weary pages were looking gray and ratty by now.) On the other hand, Cooke had actually said that its quality was not as bad as novels that had been published. But what really stunned me was the form of censorship that allowed the fear of political pressure to keep a book from being printed. I was naive enough to be shocked. Only later did I realize that such "prior restraint" is a major factor in publishing, and that it is the fears and prejudices of editors which determine what we will read, no matter what the Constitution guarantees about freedom of the press.

But Cooke had offered that glimmer of hope! Try writing something else; he promised he would give my next submittal his closest attention.

At that time, I wrote fiction slowly. I was working as a reporter on a suburban weekly newspaper, newly married, and still thumping out my prose on that battered old Smith-Corona portable. It was a durable machine, but not a kind one. It spelled poorly. It required a heavy hand to make keys strike the paper and leave a legible imprint. Not for many years would I graduate to an electric typewriter, and then an IBM Selectric, and finally to the Displaywriter word processor which I am using to write this essay.

When you work all day at reporting and writing, sometimes much longer than an eight-hour shift, among the last things you feel like doing once you get home is sitting at another typewriter and trying to coax fresh words out of your tired brain. I vowed to write a novel for Don Cooke that he could publish. But it was going *very* slowly.

I changed jobs and moved away from Philadelphia. The United States, as part of its participation in the scientific researches to be undertaken during the International Geophysical Year, announced that it would launch a series of artificial satellites. Science ficiton was starting to come true. I talked myself into a job with the Martin Co. (later to become Martin Marietta), which was building the satellite launching rocket at its plant in Middle River, Maryland, a few miles outside Baltimore. My wife and I took up residence a five-minute drive from the Martin plant and I became a Junior Technical Editor on Project Vanguard.

I watched my first novel turn into history. The Russians launched Sputnik and Americans launched one of their periodic episodes of breast-beating.

The first attempt to orbit a Vanguard satellite exploded four feet above the launching stand. Wernher von Braun and his team put up the first American satellite three months after Sputnik, and two months later we got a Vanguard satellite into orbit—with a St. Christopher's medal welded to the rocket's guidance system by the Jewish engineer who headed up the project's electronics group.

But before all that happened, two events of major significance to me personally took place. During the summer of 1956, while I sweated away at my desk on the Vanguard project (because our desks were jammed into a loft in a Martin manufacturing building, over machinery that used molten aluminum and beneath rafters that housed dive-bombing pigeons) I received a telephone call from David Kyle. He introduced himself as the chairman of the World Science Fiction Convention, which was to be held that Labor Day weekend in New York City. Could I get a couple of Vanguard engineers to come to the convention and give a presentation to the eagerly-anticipating science fiction fans?

I had never heard of science fiction fandom; this was my first inkling that people who enjoyed science fiction held conventions every year. Up until then, I had merely *read* science fiction and attempted to write it. I happily corralled the two top engineers on Vanguard and, with a little persuasion by Martin's public relations officers, got them to agree to go to New York with me. They were very nervous about the whole thing, but I assured them that they would find an audience that was seriously interested in what we were doing. When we got to the Biltmore Hotel, the first thing we saw a giant movie poster advertising some monster flick. The engineers turned to run. It took a mighty effort on my part to keep them at the convention long enough to make their presentation—which turned out to be rather boring.

Thanks to David Kyle's invitation, though, I met Arthur C. Clarke, Willy Ley, and Isaac Asimov: three first-magnitude stars in my private constellation. Clarke was at that time engaged in writing a book on the Vanguard project, which we all believed, naively, would be "man's first step into space." He was planning to visit the Martin factory soon, and was glad of the opportunity to meet a "friendly native guide."

Clarke came to Middle River and I escorted him through the project for two glorious days. The first evening, when I had to drive him to his hotel in downtown Baltimore, a hideously thick fog blew in from Chesapeake Bay and blanketed Route 40. As I inched my trusty Chevrolet along the highway, barely able to make out the hood ornament, Arthur chattered happily about some of the *real* fogs he had experienced in London.

Of course, I did what every would-be writer does. I gathered up the tattered old manuscript of my original novel, handed the shoebox of it to Arthur as he was leaving Balitmore, and implored him to read it and tell me what was wrong with it. That dear man not only took the manuscript all the way back to Ceylon with him, but he read it and sent me a letter carefully pointing out all the things that were wrong with it—but with enough encouragement thrown in, here and there, to renew my determination to write a new novel and sell it to Don Cooke.

So I sat down and started writing a novel that was set so far in the future that neither Joe McCarthy nor anyone in the next three centuries could object to it. I structured the novel shamelessly on Charles Lamb's biography of Alexander the Great, turning ancient Greek history into a super-epic of interstellar war and empire.

And, without quite realizing it, starting the saga of The Others.

That novel was titled *The Star Conquerors*. Cooke published it, all right, and it has been translated into many foreign languages. It is as out-and-out a blood-and-thunder adventure as you can imagine, so much so that I have evolved a running joke about it. Whenever a science fiction fan asks me about *The Star Conquerors*, or tells me that it was the first science fiction novel he or she ever read, I ask if I can buy back their copy of the book. It is *such* a "thud-and-blunder" novel, I claim, that I am trying to recall all the copies and get rid of them.

In truth, *The Star Conquerors* is far from my best work. There are passages in it that I would dearly like to forget about—or at least rewrite. But it holds within its pages this basic idea about The Others, the idea that there was an earlier human civilization, eons ago, which reached out toward the stars, only to be smashed almost to extinction by a superior alien race, The Others. The implacable enemy of humankind. The race that caused the Ice Age, a million years ago, with the intent of making even our homeworld of Earth unlivably hostile to us.

In *The Star Conquerors*, the saga of The Others is taken up in mid-stream (sort of the way George Lucas, many years later, started the "Star Wars" series in the middle). The people of Earth have reached the stage of interstellar colonization once again. They have established a Terran Confederation (corny, I know) among the nearer stars, rather as the city-states of ancient Greece had established colonies through the Aegean world. The Terrans know that The Others are out there, somewhere among the stars, waiting to smash us back into nothingness once again. When they encounter and are attacked by a huge alien interstellar empire, they assume it is The Others and prepare for a death struggle. If you see parallels between ancient Greece and the Persian Empire, so be it.

In *The Star Conquerors* the good guys win their war, naturally. But they learn that the aliens they

fought against are not The Others—they were merely
tools used by The Others. The real enemy is still
out there somewhere, unseen but very much feared.
The next step in the saga was *Star Watchman*,
which shows how the "victorious" Terrans deal
with the problems of running an interstellar empire.
Then came *The Dueling Machine*, in which the
problem of The Others was subordinated to a plot
dealing with the internal social stresses that forced
the Empire to reconstitute itself into a more
democratic, less tightly-controlled Commonwealth.
I was also writing nonfiction along the way,
including my first astronomy book, *The Milky Way
Galaxy*, which started as the background research
for the novels.

But that old first novel of mine would not leave
my mind. Even though the first flight to the Moon
soon enough became history instead of science
fiction, the character of Chet Kinsman and what he
stood for refused to lie still. Eventually I wrote
Millennium, and was pleased to give the first copy
of the novel off the press to Arthur Clarke—who
professed not to remember reading that awful early
manuscript. "Read your manuscript!' he snorted.
"I never read other people's manuscripts!" He
even gave me a copy of his form letter which
clearly states that he never reads other people's
manuscripts. Later, I gathered together some of
the short stories I had written about Kinsman and
used them as the backbone for a novel about his

early life, titled *Kinsman*. Sometime soon I will combine those two books, *Kinsman* and *Millennium*, rewriting them from start to finish into the definitive "biography" of the man who has inhabited my mind since 1949.

But this is supposed to be about *As On a Darkling Plain*, isn't it?

By the mid-Sixties I had written three novels and a few short stories dealing with The Others. As I said earlier, I followed no rigid plan, no preset outline. Rather, I used the basic idea of The Others and their destruction of the earlier human interstellar empire (and creation of the Ice Age) as a loose sort of environment in which to place stories. I never tried to connect one tale closely with any other; that would have been too confining.

But the saga had no beginning, as yet. What about a novel that deals with the stunning moment when the human race finds, not only that we are not alone in the universe, but that there is a superior alien intelligence that is implacably hostile to us?

I was mulling these thoughts when, at a science fiction convention, Frederik Pohl showed me a cover sketch for a future issue of *Galaxy* magazine and asked me if I would like to write a story around it. I was highly flattered. Fred was winning Hugo awards with great regularity for *Galaxy* and its companion magazine, *If*, in those years. Judy-Lynn Benjamin was his associate editor, and Lester Del Rey the managing editor. Those two would eventually marry and found Del Rey books, one of the most successful publishers of science fiction in the history of the business.

I wrote the novelet for Fred, based in part on the cover sketch, but more heavily on the ideas I had been kicking around about The Others. Sidney Lee, a minor character in *The Star Conquerors*, became the central figure now. The story was published in the January 1969 issue of *Galaxy* under the title, ''Foeman, Where Do You Flee?'' It was Fred's title, not mine; I still dislike it, but apparently I thought so little of my original title that it no longer comes to mind.

That novelet became the kernel from which *As On a Darkling Plain* grew. I added to the novel another ingredient, the idea of a lovers' triangle based on the time dilation effect of star travel, in which one member of the triangle stays on Earth and ages normally while the other two fly to Sirius at relativistic speed, and return to Earth decades younger than the stay-at-home.

One other ingredient went into *Darkling Plain*: the question that is expressed by the juxtaposition of the Haldane and Clarke quotes at the beginning of the novel. Are there limits to our ability to understand the universe? Is it ''queerer than we *can* imagine?'' Or can our minds encompass whatever we find in the vast depths of cosmic space? Clearly, the problem posed by the alien machines, and by the lurking presence of The

Others themselves, is a test not only of our ability to understand, but of our ability to survive, as well.

There you have the beginning of the saga of The Others, written a decade after the first novels in the saga appeared.

In the novel *Orion* we see the culmination of the saga. We are brought face-to-face, at last, with The Others—although we may not recognize them as such right away. Because the saga of The Others is an organic evolution, rather than a mechanical serial, *Orion* is very different from *As On a Darkling Plain*. There are no one-to-one explanations. The reader has to do some thinking, some imagining, to see how the two ends of the saga fit together. Alternatively, because *Orion* was not written as the final chapter in a tightly interlocked series, it can be read entirely on its own, with no fore-knowledge of other works necessary—as, indeed, *As On a Darkling Plain* can be read by and of itself.

One final note about *Orion*. If you should read it (or have already read it) you will notice that it is very different in nature from *As On a Darkling Plain*. Where *Darkling Plain* is straight, "hard core" science fiction based on Einstein's relativity and solid anthropological principles, *Orion* appears to be more of a fantasy, dealing with time travel, superheroes, and even gods and goddesses. Yet the physics in *Orion* is just as valid as that in any other novel of mine: the discoveries in quantum dynamics and cosmology have opened new doors for the science fiction writer, doors that lead to time travel and all its inherent paradoxes and beauties.

So, here you have the beginning of the saga of The Others. In *Orion* you have the culmination—but not necessarily the end! There are plenty of additional stories about The Others to be told. Perhaps we will all travel through time again to see them unfold.

Ben Bova
West Hartford, Connecticut

BEN BOVA